FAR SCAPE™

DARK SIDE OF THE SUN

FARSCAPE™

DARK SIDE OF THE SUN

Andrew Dymond

TOR®

A TOM DOHERTY ASSOCIATES BOOK
NEW YORK

This is a work of fiction. All the characters and events portrayed in this book are either products of the author's imagination or are used fictitiously.

FARSCAPE: DARK SIDE OF THE SUN

Copyright © 2000 The Jim Henson Company Limited.

A Tor Book
Published by Tom Doherty Associates, LLC
175 Fifth Avenue
New York, NY 10010

www.tor.com

Tor® is a registered trademark of Tom Doherty Associates, LLC.

ISBN: 0-765-34001-1

First Tor edition: September 2001

FARSCAPE™

DARK SIDE OF THE SUN

PROLOGUE

Re's collective mind reached out, probing and exploring, ranging through the depths of its aquatic world. Searching. It flickered across the dark, still ocean bed, lightly touching the rugged underwater mountains, the peaks of which rose up towards the dark rock skin that covered the surface of the planet and the vast sea. It lingered in huge, empty, black caverns, rippling over dead reefs, fondling the fossilized bones and shells of long-extinct entities, licking the languid sandbanks and shoals, restlessly seeking some response. And, as Re feared, finding none.

Its world had once pulsed with teeming life, reverberated with the sounds of birth, struggle, love, war, and death. It had been home to a seemingly infinite number of species, from simple, minute organisms, incapable of even rudimentary thought, to large, complex creatures with commensurately large, agile and devious brains—creatures that had vied with Re for supremacy, challenged it for dominance. Now its home was quiet and empty. Now Re alone remained.

Re's world was dying. And Re knew why. Re's sun, source of light and warmth, source of life itself, was approaching its own death. Massively bloated, it had become a supergiant, swelling to hundreds of times its original size. Soon it would exhaust its nuclear core, become increasingly unstable and explode, go supernova.

Re was ambivalent about its fate. Re felt guilt—indeed, it knew it deserved to die—because of what it had brought about so long ago. Yet Re longed to be given the opportunity to live and somehow make amends. No entity, not even the strange gestalt that knew itself as Re, embraces death.

Re's mind soared further afield, far beyond the sea, up through the thin crust of rock that roofed the ocean, beyond the gravitational pull of its planet, beyond the poor, thin atmosphere, beyond even the dead solar system it alone inhabited. Re's mind was open now to the constant susurrus of space, alive to the murmurs, mumbles, chirrups, rants, and cries of impossibly alien beings. Nimbly, Re rode wave after wave of broadcast messages, rapidly sifting the endless information, discarding and ignoring what was of no use—the trivial and the profound, the callow and the poignant alike—for what it sought: hope.

And when, against all odds, Re finally found it, elation quickened within. Haltingly and uneasily, Re embarked upon the unfamiliar ritual of communication with the life force, asking delicately, diplomatically, if what Re wanted was possible. The brusque, peremptory reply made it clear that it was. Salvation was possible.

But there was a price. Re understood little of material matters. What could Re possibly offer the godlike being that could, it said confidently, save them? Re's was a world with little now but rock and water, and Re was unaware of its own very particular talents and abilities and what they could be valued at; unaware that there was such a thing as a market for them. Worth, trade, negotiation, and barter were concepts Re only dimly understood. Yet Re knew that it would have to master them, if Re was to survive.

Ever careful, ever diplomatic, Re asked further questions of the being and stored away the abrupt answers. It appeared that these matters were not so difficult to understand after all. One entity wanted something and that entity gave another entity something the other entity wanted in exchange. Re wanted to leave its world. The being could facilitate that. But the being wanted something that Re did not have. The trade could not take place.

Re withdrew its mind and went back to the sterile and profound silence it had inhabited for millennia, away from the tumult, chaos, and boisterous anarchy of space, to ponder what it had learned, to consider what it must do. This was a bitter thing for Re—to be given hope, and then to lose it.

Re brooded and waited.

CHAPTER 1

Moya lay quietly in space, listening to the stars—the regular beat of the pulsars, the strange whispers of ancient giants, and the awful silence of black holes.

She had tried to ignore the problem, hoping that it would just go away. But it hadn't. For some time now, she'd been aware that something wasn't right inside, but now great waves of pain were rolling through her—convulsing her; confusing her. She shuddered and gave in. She was seriously ill.

Moya cut her main drive and simply drifted, the light of distant suns reflecting from her skinsteel hull in an ever-changing kaleidoscope of color. She didn't know what was wrong and she was frightened. She had lived a very long time—never established Moya's age—and in all that time nothing had hurt her this badly. She cut even the weak thrust of her station-keeping fields; she couldn't sustain it. Moya hoped that if she just stayed still for a while, everything would settle down and she'd be able to continue.

Then pain lanced through her flank, rolled along her nerve endings, and exploded in her brain. Something was wrong. Very, very wrong.

Inside Moya, John Crichton hummed tunelessly as he flossed. The dentics Zhaan had given him felt and tasted disgusting as they crawled over his palate, but he couldn't deny that they did their job. The toothache he had been suffering from recently was at last beginning to calm down as the little creatures ingested the infected flesh.

Inside his mouth the dentic shuddered and ceased moving. Crichton stopped humming, reached into his mouth and peeled the dentic from his lower palate. It was a shame that the dentics had to die. But consuming infection was what they were bred for.

He deposited this, his ninth dead dentic this week, into the biomatter recycler in his quarters, took a long gulp of water and gargled. He would have preferred a shot of decent malt whisky, but anything would do. Anything to take away the taste of dead dentic.

It was now nearly seven months since Crichton had first set foot aboard Moya. And he found it difficult to believe that it was indeed barely half a year since the wormhole had opened in high Earth orbit and blasted him across time and space to who-knew-what part of the universe.

He missed his family and friends. But now he had new friends and, in place of his father, he had Moya. And he liked his new friends, liked them much more than he had once thought possible. Of course, he'd never admit it—after all, that would blow his cool completely—but there were times when he found himself actually having fun on this madcap ride through the galaxy. And he was learning, too. He was a scientist, an astronaut, and he had been presented with a tremendous adventure and a great opportunity. He had left the world of his birth and he had encountered new life. And he was the first human to do it.

Crichton closed the zipper on his jumpsuit and pulled on his boots. They were handmade, crafted for durability and guaranteed for a lifetime, but the tread was already half gone. The boots were made for space flight, not walking. And certainly not for adventuring on the number of planets that he had visited over the past months.

He knew that if he told his story back home on Earth, he would be ranked alongside Marco Polo and Robert Falcon Scott. Though they were separated by centuries, he felt a deep affinity with such men. For the journeys and perils faced by those great explorers—along the silk road and across the ice of the Antarctic—though bold adventures in their own time, were merely the first nervous steps on the journey he'd undertaken. Polo and Scott had gone to the ends of the Earth. Crichton had stepped beyond it.

If he was honest, Crichton had no problem with the image of himself as an adventurer. But the truth was that, as an adventurer, he was more Robinson Crusoe than Christopher Columbus. And it was a very strange beach indeed that he had been washed up on. There may have been no Man Friday, but there was a strange and enigmatic priest, a fearsome warrior who had been framed for murder, an opportunistic, thrill-seeking thief, a deposed ruler of billions, and an undeniably attractive Peacekeeper who had been exiled by her own people.

And they were all at large in a galaxy none of them could call home, travelling in a self-aware, organic spacecraft big enough to flatten Manhattan if she chose to land on it.

The universe regarded them as curios.

The Peacekeepers hunted them as criminals.

Crichton now called them friends. Just.

He took an extraordinary joy in the wonders and terrors he had seen and lived through during these last seven months, but there were days when being the only human on a living starship the size of Manhattan could really suck. Today was one such day. He knew that if the queen of Spain were to pay him a bounty for the discovery of new worlds, he'd be the richest man alive. But he'd still have a toothache.

Crichton sighed as he cracked the seal on a new pod, extracted the incubating dentic and attached it carefully to the inside of his mouth. Clothing secure, beard dealt with and toothache under control, if not actually cleared up, he left his bedroom and entered the chamber that he called his lounge. He looked around.

The floor and walls were made of a rubbery skin-like material, threaded with veins and pulsing with life. Skinsteel gratings emerged from the floor and furniture grew from the walls. Moya had been bred for functionality, but not necessarily a human aesthetic. The floor pulsed, deep blue and red, the healthy colors of oxygen transportation.

Crichton moved to his mantelpiece—well, the shelf Moya had grown when trying to fulfil his specifications

for the room. Having a mantelpiece in a living spaceship might have seemed a pretension on any other
day . . . but not today. Crichton ran his fingers lightly
across the shelf, picked up the framed photograph.

"Hi, Dad." His voice held a hint of sadness.

The photograph came from his module, *Farscape I*,
the experimental vehicle he had been piloting when he
tore through a wormhole. His personal payload. Something that he was very glad he had brought along. Now
he was surprised at how foreign the plastic of the
frame felt to his fingers. Too other world. Too . . .
human.

And his father's face, so much like his own—the
strong brow, the clear eyes and alert, inquisitive expression. It seemed unfamiliar now . . . the face, almost, of a stranger.

How fast they fade, he thought to himself. *How
quickly we adapt.*

Feeling that confronting his sadness was the best
way to banish it, Crichton took his MiniDisc recorder
from his pocket and checked the remaining recording
time on the disc. Thirty seconds. He sighed. There
went the last thirty seconds of ZZ Top's *Afterburner.*

Crichton finalized the disc, punched in the final
chapter. His own voice filled the room. *"Hey, Dad.
Your favorite son here with another exciting instalment
of Starman Jones. This week's episode is the one where
our hero lands on a war-torn planet and ends up leading the downtrodden rebels in a futile but heroic fight
against the oppressive state. On the way he learns
about himself and comes out a better man."* Crichton
hit pause and sighed. How close had he come to erasing
every entry he had ever made? How many times had he

wondered at the futility of these silly messages to a man he would in all likelihood never see again?

Lacking an answer he elected to listen to the rest of the entry. Get it out of his system once and for all. His thumb shifted again and he heard himself say, *"Dad, you know what? In many ways, space isn't that different from home. I've been here for a few months, and guess what? Conflicts. War. Class struggles. Discrimination. There's smuggling and slavery and drugs—all patrolled by a shoot first, ask questions later intergalactic police force called Peacekeepers."*

The taped voice went on. *"Anyway, I bet you can guess that I'm feeling a little down. Low, even. You know, I've been thinking about a gift . . . and, well, last month we visited a planet. Uyani Prime. Horrible place. Mostly coal. Black seas. No industrialization. Coal went out of fashion here a long time ago. But Moya needed to eat. Compressed carbon is a delicacy to her, so the crew let her feed on as much coal as she could handle. And can she pack it away! Still, what do you expect from a living starship that's about the size of Manhattan? Anyway, I got to stretch my legs, explore the coast a bit."* There was a pause. Crichton's voice grew hushed with excitement. *"I found a fossil, Dad. You've got to see this thing. It's beautiful. Perfectly preserved. Something like an ammonite but with arms. I can see hints of skin. The detail is incredible. I've got it here in the ship. I had to leave it in the cargo bay. It's a bit big. Actually, it's six and a half meters wide. Took all six of us here to get it aboard. The thing must weigh a quarter of a ton. Aeryn nearly lost an arm. It must be a billion years old."* Crichton paused, then heard himself wonder aloud, *"I wonder what race*

*it evolved into? What heights they might have
climbed? What goals they might have achieved?
Where they are now? It's only now, out here on the
edge of the infinite, that I'm really beginning to realize
what we have back home. All I had . . . and all I lost."*
Another pause. *"Dad, I guess we both know you may
never see this beautiful example of life from another
world. I just wanted you to know I was thinking of you
on your—birthday. Happy birthday, Dad."*

Crichton clicked off the recorder. Pulling a small
wallet from another pocket he riffled through the stack
of discs contained within. Rock. Jazz. Garage. Hard-
house. His last link with Earth. Music he might never
hear again. Erasing these recordings was a sacrifice.

Talking to Dad was worth it.

Selecting Springsteen's *Born in the U.S.A.*, Crichton
loaded the disc and hit *format*, then *record*.

"Hey, Dad, your ever-lovin' blue-eyed son here.
And this week our hero's got a toothache. That'll teach
me to floss, right? They do it here with worms. Little
skinny ones that stre-e-e-tch. And dentics eat the bac-
teria around your teeth and gums. Neat, huh? Remind
me to tell you how they deal with constipation here
someday." Crichton paused. Pink goo oozed from a
fleshy tube onto a thin plate. "Hey, Dad, gotta dash.
That knock at the door was room service. The cham-
pagne here's to die for."

Crichton put away the recorder and scooped up the
first mouthful of breakfast. The pink goo tasted right—
buttered waffles and coffee—but it was annoying that
the temperature of each flavor was exactly the same—
something he had never gotten used to. And how he

missed hash browns, crisp bacon, and scrambled eggs.

Someone tapped on the skinsteel door to his quarters.

"Yeah, Aeryn. That you?"

"The very same."

The answer was not strictly necessary. Aeryn was the only member of Moya's crew who had ever thought to play the friendly neighbor. Which was odd, considering the fact that she spent 90 percent of most days either flaming mad or putting on a real good show for the natives.

Crichton, welcoming the distraction, left his breakfast and joined Aeryn in the access artery.

"I was just planning to take a turn around the block," he said. *Keep it casual.*

"Oh?"

Was that avoidance?

"And . . . I wondered if you . . ."

Crichton ventured a grin. It didn't hurt too much. "I was dressed like a million dollars and didn't care who knew it."

Aeryn looked quizzical.

"Mickey Spillane. You need a translation?"

"Please."

Crichton chuckled. "Up, dressed and rarin' to roll. You need a translation?"

"No, that will do."

They set off along the spongy floor of Moya's port-prime-access artery, heading for the cargo hold. The astronaut couldn't feel the texture of the floor beneath his feet but he knew what it was: bio-organic skinsteel threaded with veins and pulsing with the flow of blood and oxygen to Moya's vital organs.

Aeryn strode along beside Crichton, dark eyes brooding, footprints fading from the skinsteel floor behind them. To Crichton, Aeryn was a storm front running before the wind, sidewinder emotions bursting out at every opportunity to explore her new life in exile. Passionate, intelligent, opinionated; yet somehow naive, somehow . . . vulnerable. A woman of extremes and opposites, at once compellingly attractive and insanely annoying. A soul in conflict with her background and life-experience, trying to make sense of a universe that, for her, since being deemed irreversibly contaminated by her Peacekeeper captain, surely must seem to have gone mad.

"Haven't seen you around the hood for a while. Where you been hangin'?"

Aeryn tossed her thick, black hair. "Working."

"Yeah?"

"We're not all just passengers here."

"Yeah, I'm gettin' that. I just thought we might have, you know, hung for a while, that's all."

"Crichton, you're a rock-hopper." Aeryn's voice was clipped . . . hard edged.

"You weren't born in space. You can't possibly understand what it's like to live out here, beyond the confines and restrictions of a single world. It gives you a different perspective."

Crichton shook his head. "It gives me the willies."

Aeryn stopped in her tracks. Like her speech, her movements were often abrupt. "Why is it that whenever we have an opportunity to talk, you have to make sexual references?"

"What?" Crichton spun to face her. The heel of his

space boot dug a shallow gully in the floor, which seemed to fill almost magically.

"Willies." Aeryn said with vague distaste. "Isn't that a reference to . . . you know. Human reproductive . . . you *know!*"

Crichton sighed, rubbed a hand through his hair and shook his head. "I thought these bugs could handle contextual references."

"They can. But they're not infallible. And they've never had to deal with a human before."

"Oh, yeah? And what's so different about us? We're just folk. We have brains don't we? You know—that lumpy bit at the top of our central nervous systems?"

"Humans. Brains." Aeryn weighed the thought carefully. "A matter for conjecture."

Crichton let out an irritated breath. She always did this to him. You'd have thought he'd have learned by now.

"Aeryn, I'll tell you what: you keep your notions of humans to yourself and I'll go back to scratching pictures on cave walls with burnt sticks. That suit ya?"

"If we ever find a planet with caves." Aeryn's lips barely moved; the perfect deadpan.

"Whatever." Crichton was wearying of the conversation.

"And sticks."

"Yes." *Go away!* "And sticks."

Aeryn smiled, a sly expression that crept almost unnoticed across her face. "And an atmosphere capable of supporting combustion. And geological processes that support the production of sulphur for a catalyst. And . . ."

"Man! Some days you're real hard work, you know that?"

"Really?" Aeryn affected disinterest as they moved along the corridor. She had never been one to worry what others thought of her. Direct. Straightforward. Determined. These traits had been coded into her at birth; the perfect Peacekeeper mix. How her birth fellow PKs must have puzzled when Crais deemed her irreversibly contaminated because of her contact with Crichton, an alien. Within moments, her life as she knew it was over.

And so she had lost everything. Her ship, her status, her identity. An exile now, wandering the trackless gulf between stars she had once called home. If only they knew the truth. About Crais and his obsession with Crichton.

A curious mixture, this human, who was often so difficult to understand.

Crichton. Fascinating symbol of otherness. Aeryn studied the human closely. His face was set in angry lines . . . eyes narrowed as he moved . . . breath coming faster and shallower than normal. Aeryn nodded, assembling the evidence. "Tooth still troubling you?"

Crichton rubbed a finger along his lower jaw and winced. "Good guess."

"See what you get if you don't dentic regularly?"

"Jeez, Aeryn, those dentics may feed off everything from gangrene to the common cold, but to be honest," Crichton punctuated his words with a heartfelt shudder, "I'd rather floss with Rygel's nasal hairs."

Aeryn frowned in disgust. "Really?"

"Hell, no. But you know what I mean."

"You mean you want a—what do you call it—a

toothbrush? A plastic stick with abrasive hairs that can actually cause more damage than they prevent?"

Eyes closed, lost in blissful memories, Crichton replied, "Mine had nylon bristles. And a rotating head. And rechargeable batteries." His expression became dreamy. "The Formula One of oral hygiene."

Aeryn's expression of disgust deepened. "You put an electrical device in your *mouth?*"

"Oh, yes."

Aeryn sighed. "Well, it's your choice, I suppose. Not to dentic, I mean. But you should really take more care of yourself, you know that, don't you? Personal hygiene can be of paramount importance to out-worlders, and not just because of the smell. Space is full of radiation. Biological mutations happen all the time."

"And the nearest Colgate *Plaque-Defender* is several million parsecs away." Crichton surrendered to the pain long enough to whimper. "At least."

By now Crichton and Aeryn had traversed the main artery and turned into a curving side-branch. The walls here were a deeper blue, threaded with pulsing veins and well-oxygenated clumps of lumoss, which reacted to their presence by brightening as they approached and dimming as they passed.

"You still planning to—what was it you said? 'Take a turn around the block'?"

"Not likely. The way I feel at the moment I'd probably wind up doing the sidewalk shuffle with an asteroid."

Aeryn shook her head. The words were familiar, but the meaning, as usual, eluded her.

"I'll probably just spring the toolbox, have me a lit-

tle grease-monkey mojo. Try to take my mind off . . .
you know." Crichton touched the tip of one finger tenderly to his jaw.

"Grease-monkey . . . mojo?"

"Sure, you know. Drain the sump. Polish the pistons."

The light suddenly dawned for Aeryn. "You
mean . . . service the engine? Of your module?"

"Yeah. You got it."

The cargo hold brightened as the valve unpinched to
allow them entry. Lumoweed growing from the vaulted
chamber roof began to crawl towards them, attracted to
their body heat, converting the energy to visible light.

The module was parked at the base of a fuelling
root, battered but unbowed. Loosely based on a space
shuttle design, it was sleeker and smaller, with dispro-
portionately large engine housings. It had been these
highly experimental engines that had cracked open a
wormhole in Earth orbit and blasted Crichton halfway
across the universe.

Crichton ran a finger along one of the many scars in
the module's ceramic composite hull. The scar
stopped short at one of three oval system upgrade
modules grafted seamlessly onto the bow. Crichton
placed his palm flat against the scar, careful to touch
only the original . . . the part that had been built on
Earth. His lips curled in a half-smile.

*Dad running his good-luck wash leather across the
pilot's canopy. Himself sneaking up with the pressure
hose. The grin on Dad's face. The granddaddy of all
water fights, out there on the steaming concrete under
a broiling sun. A way to forget. A way to wash away
the pain of separation . . . of loss . . . even if only for a
few moments.*

" 'Ran every red light down Memory Lane. . . . ' "
Crichton's depressed whisper echoed something his
father had once said. He glanced sideways at Aeryn.
"Dire Straits," he added by way of clarifying the
lyric.

Aeryn followed Crichton's fingers along the scar in
the hull. "You were in trouble?"

A snort of laughter pushed aside the memories. "A
covers band."

"Banned? What from? And why would it need
covering?"

"Nah, a *band*. Talk about being divided by a common language. You know. Rock, baby. I want my
MTV." Crichton mimed a passable air-guitar solo. . . .

"MTV? Why would you want a Modular Terraforming Vehicle? There are no rocks on Moya. Air, water
and accommodation are free."

Crichton grinned, then winced and cupped his face
with a hand. "Man, it hurts when I laugh." He un-
dogged *Farscape*'s canopy and reached behind the
pilot's seat to the stowage locker. The toolbox was
scuffed plastic, covered with passport stickers. Rome.
Paris. Tokyo. Olympus. Extracting the toolbox, he entered a code sequence into the dash-comp. The three
upgrade modules unpinched with a nicely harmonized
nasal wheeze.

"You're going to modify a custom-grown starflight
systems upgrade module with . . ." Aeryn regarded the
open toolbox disdainfully, ". . . what have you got in
there, anyway?"

Crichton shrugged. "Some doodads I picked up on
my travels. Never know when you might need to
tweak a widget here, a grommet there." He looked up.

Aeryn was wearing her impatient face again. "You never go hot-rodding?"

Aeryn waited for an explanation.

"Guess not." Crichton weighed up the tools then made his selection.

"So, is the pain from your tooth really bad?"

"Good segue," Crichton deadpanned as he levered himself onto the hull and stuck his head and shoulders into the upgrade module. "And before you ask, that's a musical bridge. And since you ask, yeah, the pain's . . . well, it's a pain."

"Sharp or dull?"

"Both." His reply was muffled.

"Sensitive?"

"Mmmm. Temperature and pressure. I'm on a tepid soup diet." Crichton emerged from the module long enough to grab a new tool from the kit. "Why so interested?"

"I'm only trying to help."

"I think it's an abscess." His voice became muffled again and partly obscured by banging noises. "The right side of my face feels like it's on fire. My ear feels like it's full of goo. I keep wanting to grind my teeth. And when I do . . ."

"Did you see Zhaan?"

"Sure."

"And?"

"She gave me a bigger dentic."

"Good. Did you use it?"

"Sure." What Aeryn could see of Crichton's body shuddered at the memory.

"And?"

"It died."

"It died?"

"Well, yeah. I mean, it stopped, you know, wriggling around in there. Tasted foul. And it smelled." A thought. "Are they supposed to do that?"

"I've never needed to use one."

"Oh."

"But I've heard they can grow to a great age if properly fed."

"Reusable dentics, huh? Well, this one took one gander at my lower right six molar and kicked the bucket."

"Kicked the bucket?"

"Gave up the ghost. Threw in the towel. You know, snuffed it. Guess my infection wasn't up to its fussy high standards or something. Say, Aeryn, are you blocking the light?"

"No."

Crichton popped his head out of the module. "Is it my imagination or is it getting dim in here?" He glanced around. Lumoweed clustered overhead, spreading itself across the fuelling root system main trunk, snuggling close in a useful but disconcertingly friendly way.

Aeryn followed his gaze. "Maybe it is a little . . ." She broke off as the lumoweed suddenly emitted a burst of brilliant white light, followed immediately by darkness.

"Ow. Jeez." Crichton rubbed colored blobs from his stunned eyes. "More pain. Thank you, Lord."

Aeryn's eyes narrowed as she cast her gaze around them. The vaulted roof flickered with pulses of sickly

light from the lumoweed. Aeryn tensed. Something
was very wrong.

Crichton opened his mouth to speak, but without
warning the floor shuddered and both Sebacean and
human fought for balance. Crichton's teeth clicked together painfully. Achingly bright blasts of light came
from the previously dark lumoss. Moya heaved again,
more violently. Crichton was thrown to the floor.

"What the frell . . . ?"

He reached out to grasp the hand Aeryn extended
towards him. The hand was warm, the skin dry, the
pressure from her fingers strong. But Crichton only
had a second to register this before he was pulled
roughly back to his feet.

Aeryn looked around. She seemed almost . . . scared.

"Something must be wrong with Moya," she said.

Pilot came in over their comms: "Moya is unwell. I
have detected the site of primary infection."

The hull shook again; Crichton struggled to keep his
balance. "Great timing, Pilot." Crichton began to retrieve the tools that he'd dropped when he'd fallen. "I
was just looking forward to a good tinker."

"Timing is regrettable. Moya is really *quite* unwell.
And she is frightened. I have detected further sites of
secondary infection."

"Something serious?"

"I regret to inform you the danger is grave. The infection is spreading quickly."

Crichton and Aeryn headed for the bridge.

Moya's bridge was a wide semicircular chamber with
a vaulted roof supported by bonelike growths. Skin-

steel coated all exposed surfaces, pulsing as Moya breathed air into the chamber for the crew to breathe. Veins threaded the walls and floor. Lumoss glowed in healthy clumps on the walls and ceiling, brightening the chamber further in response to each new occupant.

To Crichton, being inside the bridge was like being in an underwater cave. A coral cave. Sunlight, rainbow-hued fish fluttering past your mask . . . the soft sound of air pulsing in your regulator . . . constant reminders of just how alive this starship they knew as Moya really was.

And now she was ill. What if she died? Who would make their air, their food and water? How would they live? How would he get back to Earth?

Crichton told himself not to overreact. After all, how serious could it be?

The access valve to the bridge pinched shut behind them with a breathy wheeze. Everyone else was already there. Zhaan. D'Argo. Chiana. Rygel.

"Ah, Crichton and Aeryn, good. We've been waiting." Rygel's voice was imperious. After all, he was, as he never let anyone forget, Rygel XVI, Dominar of six hundred billion subjects. Not quite the embodiment of ultimate leadership. Crichton shot the small Hynerian a glance. With bulgy eyes and a glum look usually etched on his leathery face he resembled a large frog with a thyroid disorder. What Rygel lacked in height, he made up for in ego. Now his leathery body quivered in his ThroneSled, which he maintained at a height just slightly above Crichton's eye level—very important when you were only a shade over two feet tall.

Crichton studied Rygel. It was hard to read the emotion on the face of such a being. But something didn't feel right.

A movement caused Crichton to turn. Chiana had moved close, her feet silent on the skinsteel floor. White hair crowned her pixie face. Almond-shaped eyes, high cheeks, softly pouting lips. Beautiful, yes. But also a thief; a seductress; a con artist; an adrenaline junkie with bad in her blood and mischief on her mind. Crichton was mindful of Chiana—sensuality and evil in the same perfect body; the devil's gift.

Chiana lifted a hand to Crichton's shoulder, her body orbiting his, precise, dagger-sharp movements. "So nice to see you, John." Her voice was silk, but silk could strangle. With an effort, Crichton pulled himself from her touch, and looked at the rest of the crew. Pa'u Zotoh Zhaan, her smooth, blue face decorated with exotic markings . . . as befitting one evolved from vegetable rather than animal stock. And Ka D'Argo, whose bearlike presence, infrequent speech, and obsession with weapons marked him as pure animal, yet whose soul was the most sensitive of them all.

And lastly former Peacekeeper, Officer Aeryn Sun—a woman who wore fury like a cloak, kept it wrapped close at all times, her own personal shield. How attractive would she be if she ever let that cloak drop, even for a second? Crichton had an inkling of the answer.

While Crichton was attempting to size up the situation, Aeryn had been speaking quietly with Zhaan. Now she turned to look at him, silent, eyes flashing with anger. The transformation came as a complete surprise to Crichton and he frowned. *What does she know that I don't?* He racked his brain for some clue. All either of them knew for sure was that Moya was ill—and yet Aeryn now seemed to know something he didn't.

"Pilot said Moya wasn't well. What's wrong with her?"

No one answered. Crichton's frown deepened. It wasn't just Aeryn. Everyone was staring at him. Crichton shook his head wearily. "You know, when I was a kid and I did something wrong, Dad would call me into his study. He wouldn't say anything . . . he'd just look at me for a while. Wait for me to speak first. Wait to see if I could figure out what I'd done wrong before dishing out the medicine."

The only response was accusing looks, though Chiana's smile deepened with anticipation.

"Why do I get the feeling I've been summoned here for a spanking?"

"Crichton, how could you do something so stupid?" Aeryn's voice was as hard as her expression.

"Tell you what, Aeryn. You tell me what you think I did and I'll tell you if I did it. Fair?"

"You put your dead dentics into the recyclers!" she shouted.

Crichton shrugged. "So? They died. I threw them away. We talked about this already."

"You didn't tell me you *recycled* them!"

"And there's a problem with that?"

"Yes, John," Zhaan said calmly, "we have a problem when Moya converts recycled biomass into food, yes."

Crichton's face flushed. "She eats recycled waste?"

D'Argo growled. "Moya is a living ship. You thought otherwise?"

"Well, you know, I've never been on a living star-ship before . . . I mean . . . I thought, I dunno, maybe she photosynthesized or something." He threw up his hands in exasperation. "I mean, how the hell was I supposed to know?"

Aeryn's voice was scornful. "He didn't *know.*"

"For crying out loud, it's just a *toothache!*"

"Exactly." Zhaan was still calm. "A *human* infection."

"An infection that Moya could not detect and against which she has no defense," Aeryn added, angrily.

Pilot explained. "For Moya the disease pathology takes the form of what you would call 'necrotizing fasciitis.' Deadly, I'm afraid."

"Congratulations, Crichton," D'Argo snarled coldly. "This could prove fatal to Moya. And to all of us as well."

As if to prove his point, the floor convulsed. It wasn't hard to understand that Moya was suffering. Her pain hovered over the bridge like ancient ghosts, unable to rest.

CHAPTER 2

Aeryn studied the Free-Trader fleet modelled spectacularly in Moya's bridge viewtank. She noticed looks the others sent her way, but disregarded them. She wanted to remain focused on the current situation, but it was hard. Especially hard when those into whose company she had fallen often demonstrated how unfit for command they were.

Take their latest brainstorm, for instance. The decision to approach Jansz.

Shortly after the realization that Crichton's infected slug was the cause of Moya's life-threatening illness, the bridge had been silent while Crichton absorbed the full extent of his mistake.

"Necrotizing fasciitis?" His voice had been soft, disbelieving. "You mean . . ."

"That's right, Crichton." Pilot's voice, though calm, betrayed his concern. "Five percent of Moya's tissue is dead. The rate of necrotic destruction is advancing rapidly."

Aeryn had watched Crichton's face. She could almost see his mind working as he performed a rapid calculation. "Five percent. That's an area the size of a city block."

"And increasing," Pilot added.

"Is that muscle tissue, Pilot?" Aeryn wanted as much information as possible so they could formulate a plan.

"What difference does it make?" demanded D'Argo.

Aeryn sighed. "Because if it's muscle damage we only have problems with doors and other purely physical systems. If it's nerve damage . . . clearly, anything could happen." She waited for the attention she knew that her observation would get.

"I get it," Crichton said. "One good spasm from Moya and we could all be crushed. Or bounced too close to a supernova. The air supply could shut down or our food could be spiced with poison . . ."

D'Argo considered Aeryn's summary and nodded his massive skull. A slight but respectful gesture. He got the point.

"I'm afraid both muscles and nerves are affected, Officer Sun," Pilot replied. "I will, of course, keep you informed of the damage."

"This is bad." *And not only because you guys have never seen* Star Wars, Crichton thought to himself. "Is there anything we can do to halt the infection?"

Zhaan answered. "Necrotic destruction is irreversible, John. Tissue damage is the result of an enzyme imbalance caused by a viral infection. The problem is that although we can eventually identify and treat the virus, the enzyme imbalance is progressive, and cannot be stopped."

"So, it's inevitable that Moya's going to die?"

Pilot spoke again. "I have identified the primary center of damage. Moya's facia gland is damaged beyond repair."

Zhaan gasped. "That gland controls the enzyme balance in her body."

"Is that like the human hypothalamus?" Crichton asked.

"I expect so," Zhaan agreed. Her knowledge of human anatomy was limited at best. "Destruction of the organ is not in itself fatal—the inability to produce or control enzyme production in the body *is*."

"An accurate summation, Zhaan," Pilot concurred.

Aeryn had watched Crichton throughout this exchange. It had been hard for her to control herself. She wanted to lash out, to hammer some sense of reality into the pleebing idiot. Too late now, of course. Crichton really was a stupid alien. A primitive being from a primitive world. No wonder that out of a population of billions, only a few hundred humans had ever even left the atmosphere of the planet on which they lived.

Fools. Complete hingemots.

She—and the rest of the crew—had been fooled by Crichton's apparent intelligence and humor. Yes, he was a fascinating creature, and one she had considered capable of great growth. They had all wanted to believe him capable of fitting in, of learning how to be part of life in a larger universe than the one he had known . . . but this act, this—outright stupidity—why, even a *child* would know better than to do what Crichton had done.

Under the withering stares of his companions, Crichton had become defensive. "How was I to know?" he shouted. "I'm the new kid on the block. I don't know all the rules yet."

No matter whose fault, the fact remained that Moya was dying.

Crichton continued. "The point is, it's useless to place blame. None of us wants Moya to die, do we? So why aren't we trying to figure out a way of saving her?"

"You heard Zhaan," D'Argo growled. "There is no cure."

"OK, so we don't have a cure. What about someone else? Don't you guys have hospitals out here?"

"Hospitals?" D'Argo roared. "In the Uncharted Territories?"

Moya shuddered again. The skinsteel floor moved beneath their feet.

"The damage has begun to affect Moya's nervous system," Pilot reported. The neuronal sheaths are beginning to decay and, soon, some motor functions will be affected."

"Can Moya still travel?" Zhaan asked.

"Barely . . . but yes."

"Good. Is she able to detect transmissions?"

"Yes."

"Good. Have Moya search the midrange hyperwave bands for this signature."

Zhaan pronounced a complex code-set

"That's a Free-Trader wavelength," said Aeryn angrily.

Zhaan nodded calmly. "Yes, it's Jansz's wavelength."

D'Argo's eyes narrowed suspiciously.

Chiana's eyes widened with interest.

Crichton looked puzzled.

"Free-Traders! Are you magra-fahrbot?" shouted Rygel, working himself into a royal rage. "That blotching trader Jansz can't be trusted! I'd like to blast the crank out of them all!"

"Don't be absurd, Rygel. Moya is not armed, remember?" Zhaan reminded him.

"A situation that should be remedied at the earliest possible opportunity," muttered the Hynerian Dominar.

"I've seen what these pirates can do firsthand," Aeryn interjected. "And Jansz is the worst of the lot. Why seek him out?"

"Jansz may be a buccaneer and a liar and a cheat . . ."

"And a murderer and a torturer!" Rygel insisted.

"Perhaps."

"Hhmmp! No *perhaps* about it. They're all the same, these . . ."

"But, Rygel," Zhaan continued, "he's also known to have an apothecary second only to that of a major planetary installation. If there's a cure to be found for Moya, Jansz will have it, or know where to get it."

"But what will Jansz want in exchange," D'Argo growled. "We are all fugitives. What do we have to trade that is worth our lives?" And that question put an end to the conversation.

Almost ten arns had passed since then, during which the crew had contemplated D'Argo's question. Ten arns in which Moya had limped painfully through the galaxy towards a dubious—even dangerous—rendezvous. Her systems were becoming progressively weaker as the tissue damage spread. Muscle, nerve, artery; hull, solar panels, interior hatches . . . the damage had now infected 8 percent of her body mass. And it was still spreading.

Now, at last, they had come within sight of the Free-Trader fleet. Moya managed to summon enough energy to model the spellbinding sight in the bridge viewtank. Aeryn was used to seeing large numbers of ships, but even she had not witnessed such a flotilla since the last major offensive undertaken by the Peacekeepers, three cycles before she had been banished for being declared contaminated.

Backlit by the swirling aurora of a spiral nebula, more than a hundred ships ran before the solar wind howling from a nearby blue supergiant star. No two ships were the same size or shape. Each displayed its own colors in a blaze of running lights. Neon graffiti hull tattoos shone in the darkness. A nomad culture on the move, the flotilla was also lit by continual rainbow flashes as individual vessels arrived or departed from the fleet. A gestalt entity in which the whole was far more than just the sum of the parts.

Pride. Defiance. Independence. This was how the Free-Traders defined themselves.

Hundreds of shuttles moved between the larger ships. Message pods, personnel and cargo transports; passenger yachts; guide markers; sensor drones; weapons buoys.

The flotilla spread itself across more than eighty degrees of the forward view. Its population clearly rivalled that of a large planetary city. Before its iridescent bulk Moya hung like a baby squid before a coral reef, skinsteel hull fluorescing with pain.

"Holy cow." Crichton simply could not keep the awe from his voice. "Holy . . . freakin' . . . cow."

"How do we approach them?" As ever, D'Argo's question was direct and to the point.

"The question may be moot." Pilot's voice was weakening. Symbiotically linked to Moya, he was beginning to show signs of the same necrotic damage that threatened the ship herself.

The viewtank image enlarged, showing a number of specks emerging from the flotilla to approach them.

"Dock skiffs," Pilot announced.

"Coming to check us out," Crichton added.

The specks enlarged rapidly, revealing themselves to be midrange vehicles with tow points and cranes. At the same time, voices came over the open channel.

"This is Ipsan Djanko of the Irulan Culture. On behalf of my clone-brothers I salute you, new trader, and ask that you take lymph-wine with us before discussing your requirements."

The crew exchanged looks.

"Polite, aren't they?" Crichton observed.

A second voice crackled into life: "Introduction of self: Squeenwhittal of Tensal IV. Request pleasure of company to discuss terms of trade. Saliva fruit and drones await."

Crichton raised an eyebrow. "And friendly."

A third voice broke in, harshly: "Maintain distance from our exclusion zone. Do not enter without express permission. Trade with the Ytaxan Conglomerate is concluded. Weapon pods are energized. Any attempt to steal the Yartarna Paloo will be met with ultimate force."

"The Yartarna Paloo, huh?" Crichton nodded, thoughtfully. "I can see right away why we'd want one of those."

And then the voices—the many, many voices—began in earnest, as the trade representatives occupying the dozens of skiffs clustered nearby began to enquire after the new business opportunity Moya clearly provided.

". . . welcome you to the most exciting and innovative . . ."

". . . treasures you no doubt seek within our . . ."

". . . promise you exclusive use of . . ."

". . . not under any circumstances listen to anyone who promises you . . ."

". . . males and females of various . . ."

". . . nonexclusive contracts . . ."

". . . competitive rates for . . ."

". . . seeds of . . ."

". . . energy weapons that . . ."

". . . practical solutions to . . ."

". . . exquisitely carved sponge idols . . ."

And on. And on.

Until, at last, a sudden, welcome silence fell and Pilot announced, "I have taken the liberty of broadcasting greetings and polite rebuttals on appropriate wavelengths."

Crichton grinned. "Good move, Pilot. Talk about the hard sell. So," he glanced from one crew member to the next, his gaze eventually resting on Zhaan. "So, how do we say 'hi!' to this Jansz character?"

Zhaan clasped her hands over the folds of her blue robe. "We wait. Eventually Jansz will come to us."

"Yeah? Seems a little passive to me. Doesn't this guy have a cell phone? Can't we call him up or something?"

"That will not be required." Zhaan seemed very sure of her words. "Jansz runs this fleet."

"His ships are the biggest and best armed," Aeryn added. "He provides protection for the traders, arbitrates all negotiations . . . and takes his cut, of course."

"I see." Crichton nodded. "Lord of the Manor."

"A feudal hierarchy seems perfectly appropriate to me," Rygel stated imperiously from the height of his ThroneSled.

Crichton grinned at Rygel. "It would, wouldn't it. You *are* a Dominar."

Rygel preened. "Aren't I?"

"Albeit a deposed one."

"Yes, well, enough of this idle chatter." Rygel squirmed uncomfortably on his ThroneSled, wringing a few more centimetres of height out of the cranky anti-gravs. "We have another visitor." A wrinkled finger pointed at the viewtank.

A skiff approached swiftly, growing larger in the viewtank. As it came nearer, the horde of acquisitive greeters scattered quickly, engines flaring as if the pilots could not get away fast enough. The skiff hove to off Moya's port flank.

Crichton studied the image. "So we do," he murmured.

Pilot opened a hyperwave transmission channel. "Introduction of self: Vurid Skanslav. Lifelong Facilitator to Trader-Prime Jansz. Vurid welcomes new traders. Is pleased to discuss business opportunities. Vurid may board?"

Vurid Skanslav was a curious sight.

To Crichton, the Facilitator resembled a scorpion

whose head had been replaced by a long muscular neck, topped by a snake-like head. Six eyes waved atop protruding stalks. He stood no more than half a meter tall at the shoulder but was more than two and a half meters in length. His back appeared to be made of a cream-colored chitinous material, with sliding plates that were dyed in complex pictograms—images Crichton took to be others of the same species in various anatomical poses, plus several rows of what appeared to be complex hieroglyphics. *So pirates even have tattoos out here,* Crichton mused, struggling to repress a grin as he wondered what the words meant. *Born To Kill? Wyld Chylde? I Love Mom?*

What Crichton assumed was a stinger arched another meter above the decorated back, and topped a snakelike tail. The cream-colored chitin of the Facilitator's neck, tail, and legs were banded with yellow-ochre zebra stripes. His belly was lightly furred, a pale yellow in color. Four arm-limbs projected forward from the main body, ending in hands with long, fully articulated fingers. Five of the six leg-limbs tapered into chitinous points. One, however, ended in a knobbed clump of scar tissue, apparently the result of a terrible wound. The fingers, arms, and legs, were all triple-jointed, allowing the Facilitator to move rapidly—in spite of a nasty limp.

The Facilitator now stood in Moya's main dock, his legs momentarily leaving shallow punctures in the skinsteel floor as he walked.

Head held high, and each eye tracking a different crew member, Vurid Skanslav studied the newcomers. Several were similar in appearance. Their voices, too, were similar, occupying a narrow bandwidth at roughly the middle of his own audible range. They wore clothing that served to confuse their gender. Vurid thought quickly. Lord Jansz would want to know exactly what the newcomers had to trade, would want a priority consideration if their cargo was valuable. But Vurid was worried. Something about these newcomers did not add up. With one exception they were too . . . anonymous. Vurid controlled his stinger. It would not do to damage negotiations before they even began. Yet he was worried. These aliens were quite odd, to say the least. It was their smells, the pheromonal signature that each gave off, that most enabled him to tell them apart.

And this only served to intensify his confusion. Each signature told a different story. Each story conflicted. Each of these creatures considered itself the dominant individual!

Why were they here?

What did they want?

What did they have to trade?

Vurid was not sure. And time was passing. Lord Jansz would want them assessed as soon as possible.

Vurid decided to take a chance. After all, chance was a prime factor in negotiations. It was a skill that, properly cultivated, Lord Jansz had been known to reward handsomely.

Addressing the smallest member of the party, the one that, perched silently atop a technologically advanced vehicle, was surely the real leader of the group, Vurid announced: "Vurid brings invitation to new traders to dine with Trader-Prime Jansz. Refreshment, conversation, entertainment guaranteed. Negotiation optional. Legal advisor available. Recommend answer in affirmative. Moonsponge wine mulled on the lava fields of Gol. Also, regret: refusal precludes trade elsewhere in fleet."

Rygel smacked his lips appreciatively. "Mulled Moonsponge wine. Perhaps my previous misgivings were overhasty."

Crichton glanced at the Hynerian. "Rygel, you're just cheap." Turning to Zhaan he asked, "Is that how trade works here?"

"Yes, John. Trade is also known to be conducted strictly according to protocol. Breach of protocol has been known to result in . . . problems."

"Legal problems?" Crichton was curious.

"Lethal problems," D'Argo clarified.

"OK, so they just made us an offer we can't refuse." Crichton turned to the Facilitator and crouched so that he was at eye level with him. "I'm for lunch and a spot of barter. Who's with me?"

CHAPTER 3

There were seats, arranged in a circle, but no table. Surprisingly, there were seven other guests for lunch.

Crichton had seen some things in his travels on Moya, but none to match this incredible display of alien life. To his left squatted three identical creatures, each resembling a six-limbed emu with sail-like growths running down their twin necks and spectacular crests of metallic blue feathers on their twin heads.

Vurid began the introductions. "Crew of Moya, pleased to introduce valued guests, AB-Eet, AB-Elit, AB-Eradigit."

The twin-headed emus nodded politely, a six-part syncopated movement that had Crichton wondering which head was A and which was B, and how they ever told the difference under all those feathers.

To their left, was a creature that could only be described as a giraffe growing out of a starfish's body.

Long-lashed, almost human eyes regarded Crichton with disturbingly frank interest.

"Valued guest, Lady Belladonna Argrave."

Starfish limbs rippled modestly and melting brown eyes fixed on Crichton. "Don't let that old stinger fool you. I'm anything but a lady." Belladonna's laugh was the sound of wind chimes.

Next around the circle was a perfect cube of what looked like crystalline iron alum. Perched on a wooden podium, the mustard-colored block was revolving slowly, deliberately, clearly surveying the Moya crew. Crichton had no idea how the block was able to see.

Vurid continued the introductions. "Albedo Point Zero Eight."

As if in reply, the mustard-colored cube pulsed a darker orange, then continued its stately and silent revolution.

Opposite Crichton were two creatures resembling winged crocodiles. The wings were folded neatly, a pose mirrored by the four-fingered hands clasped across the creatures' scaled bellies.

"Vurid's pleasure to introduce valued guests, Roahr and Graohl."

The winged crocodiles inclined their long-jawed heads. And yawned. Alarmingly. Crichton couldn't help thinking of the weapons they'd been required to leave behind before entering Jansz's ship, a traditional prenegotiation ritual. D'Argo's Qualta Blade would sure have come in handy should events get out of hand.

Next to Crichton were Aeryn, Zhaan, D'Argo, Chi-

ana, and Rygel. An empty place and then a spot for
Vurid completed the circle.

"The Compound," announced Vurid, "is pleased to
meet crew of Moya."

Vurid waited for a spokesperson from the Moya
contingent. Since his first encounter with the crew,
Vurid was having second thoughts about the esteem in
which Rygel was held by his shipmates.

"Yeah, hi. How ya doing? I'm John Crichton,
pleased to meet your good selves. From my right we
have Aeryn Sun, Pa'u Zotoh Zhaan, Ka D'Argo, Chiana, and Rygel . . ."

". . . the XVI, ruler of the Empire of . . ."

". . . Hyneria. I know, Rygel, we'll get your whole
history before the starter's done, I'm sure."

Rygel sniffed disapprovingly and urged his Throne-
Sled to a slightly greater height.

Vurid curled his body into a hoop shape. "Honored
guests. Lunch served now." Wide metal dishes were
lowered through serving hatches in the high ceiling. The
meal progressed slowly through several courses. Conversation was interesting but Crichton found himself increasingly on edge. It was all very well to make small
talk with Doctor Doolittle's menagerie, but he wanted to
get down to business. Moya was sick—and getting more
so every moment that passed. Yet the others seemed content to pass the time in idle conversation.

Three courses into the meal Crichton decided to
throw a curveball onto the field. Interrupting a conversation between Belladonna and Rygel—the subject of
which was Rygel, naturally—Crichton said bluntly, "I
thought we were invited to lunch with Jansz."

Vurid's head remained close to his platter, but his eyes swivelled to cover Crichton. "Lord Jansz here now."

Crichton nodded pointedly at the empty platter. "Conspicuous by his absence, I'd say."

Vurid made a slithery hissing noise. The emus nodded rapidly, setting their feathered crests waving like foil streamers.

"Look, under different circumstances there's nothing I'd like better than to rap with you guys. But circumstances are a little stretched right now, you with me? We've got a problem, and we've come here to trade. If no one else is willing to open that line of dialogue, I sure am."

Vurid slowly lifted his head to face Crichton. The eyes tracked independently. Human brains used two spatially displaced images to create depth of field; Crichton found himself wondering what kind of a brain you'd need to integrate six different images into a single worldview. "Lord Jansz studies new traders with more eyes than own," Vurid informed him with a slight tone of superiority. "Good for perspective."

Crichton glanced around the circle. Belladonna. The emus. Alby. The crocs. Everyone was staring at him. "Stranger in a strange land, I may be. But I don't get it, I'm afraid."

Belladonna laughed her wind-chime laugh. "How quaint! Does every—what is it you call the gestalts on your world—does every country on Earth have the same old-fashioned notion of individuality?"

Crichton frowned, looked at the rest of the crew for help. Not for the first time he was feeling a little out of his depth. Crichton couldn't help cutting to the chase. Anything else was a waste of time, a waste of life.

Zhaan explained. "John, our 'lunch guests' *are* Lord Jansz. They are his eyes and ears and mind—for now, anyway."

"Telepathy?" Crichton mulled the concept over for a moment. "That's a bit Flash Gordon, isn't it?"

"Oh, we have our own personalities as well, John Crichton," Belladonna remarked. "Could you imagine a galaxy without such sparkling conversational delicacies as your fellow luncheon guests? But from time to time Jansz chooses from among us and rents our perceptions via an affinity gene-link. He pays very well. We're peripheral components of his psyche—his Compound. In the same way that a compound eye is made of many lenses, we are Jansz's many views on new situations."

"And the empty place? I suppose that's just to allay suspicions, is it? To make us think Jansz isn't really here?"

Vurid gestured across the circle of hanging platters. "Empty place symbol for unknown. Is important factor in negotiation. Never forget, never underestimate, or bad profit is. Bad profit and death."

"And what does Lord Jansz think of his new opportunity for trade?" Crichton asked boldly.

"Not fence words. Lord Jansz knows trade required urgently. Body language, secretions, skin color, vocal traits of individual John Crichton, empathic emissions. All confirm Lord Jansz has dominant trade position." Vurid hesitated, seemed to compose himself. The Compound hung up their cutlery, allowing the implements to dangle on their chains beside their platters.

Here it comes, thought Crichton.

"Moya party state requirements. Negotiation follow if trade appeals to Lord Jansz."

"And if trade doesn't appeal?"

"Moya party free to trade with other ships. Lord Jansz will collect tithe upon completion. If completion is."

Crichton glanced at Zhaan. "Over to you, champ."

Zhaan carefully rehung her cutlery and touched her lips with a napkin before beginning. "Our need is of a medical nature. Our ship, Moya, is ill. She has an enzyme imbalance that can only be cured with specialized medical treatment. Jixit root, plintak, zaccus, and gavork, all of which I have, are of no use."

The emus cocked their heads to one side, feathers gently fluttering as the creatures studied Zhaan. Belladonna and the other members of Jansz's Compound focused on Aeryn, Chiana, D'Argo, and Crichton.

"Hormone imbalance terminal?" Vurid queried.

Zhaan glanced at D'Argo. His expression seemed to indicate that there was no point in trying to bluff. Chiana seemed to be sizing up the silverware. The little thief would snurch anything that wasn't nailed down.

• "The illness is terminal, yes. Her hormone regulating organ is almost destroyed. Necrosis is spreading throughout her body. We need—we ask—that we be allowed to consult with the most experienced apothecary in your flotilla, in the hope of finding a cure."

"Trade is—for cure, or for meeting?" asked the Facilitator.

D'Argo jumped to his feet. "Are you frelling tinked? Of course trade is for a cure!"

Zhaan remained calm. "We are willing to consider our request as a two-part trade."

Vurid shivered, and Crichton thought it must be with delight. Good for Vurid. He'd successfully maneuvered another bunch of suckers into a trade negotiation beneficial to his Lord. Inwardly, however, Crichton groaned. All this was such a waste of time! Why didn't they just state the problem, find out if there was a solution and ask the going rate? Then they could—

Crichton realized that the three ABs were staring at him, crests almost motionless.

"What . . ."

". . . value . . ."

". . . knowledge . . ."

". . . of . . ."

". . . starship . . ."

". . . illness?" The question was phrased by six mouths in such a rapid succession that they became a single chirruping voice. Crichton didn't know which creature—indeed, which head—to look at or reply to.

"What . . ."

". . . price . . ."

". . . pay . . ."

". . . for . . ."

". . . cure . . ."

". . . for . . ."

". . . starship?"

"Well that's simple," Crichton began. "Whatever we have to. Now can we get on with it? Time waits for no . . ." The Compound regarded Crichton with single-minded interest. "Well, what I mean is, time is clearly of the essence here."

"John," Zhaan interceded. "I think it might be better if you . . ."

Crichton lost patience. "You think it would be better if I what? Just shut up and let everyone keep playing their little head games? Well, let me remind you of something you may have forgotten. Moya and Pilot are dying. And you know where that puts us. And I don't mean here at the local chow-down."

"John, please be calm. Anger solves nothing. You must balance your inner and outer . . ."

"The frell with being calm, Zhaan! It's my fault and I'm not going to stand by while a bunch of hot air merchants dally over the price of a cure! Now we either start negotiations or . . ."

D'Argo laid a restraining hand on Crichton's forearm, and then tightened his fingers. Crichton knew that trying to remove the Luxan's hand from his arm would be useless. He raised his eyes to D'Argo's face. The massive Luxan held Crichton's glare with a calm stare—one Crichton had come to realize could conceal almost any emotion. The tentacles growing from his skull quivered—the only clue to his emotional state. "Listen to Zhaan. She is wise. Do not let your judgement be impaired."

"Don't be hasty, John," Zhaan added quietly. "Let's talk this through. We'll get what we want, you'll see."

Crichton pressed his lips together angrily. He glanced at Aeryn for support. Of all of them she was the one most like himself, most human. And yet there were times when she was as far from human as the galaxy in which she lived. Today was clearly such a day. Aeryn remained impassive. Crichton didn't even bother with Chiana. You'd never catch her taking up an unpopular cause. Out of all of them, she would be the one that Moya's death would affect the least. She was a survivor. She'd find a way out of this mess.

Crichton's musings were interrupted by a peculiar sensation at the back of his neck. He frowned. The last time he'd felt like this was just before the port afterburner on the prototype X-51 flamed out twenty-eight thousand feet over the Nevada desert. Never one to ignore his pilot's instinct, he glanced around. Something was wrong—no, something was . . . different.

Zhaan had noticed it too. Aeryn's eyes were scanning the room, D'Argo was shifting uncomfortably in his seat. Chiana was edgier than usual. Something was definitely up. And then Crichton realized what it was.

The seven alien lunch guests had stopped talking. They were perfectly silent. And they were all breathing exactly in time.

Vurid stood, chitin plates slithering over one another like well-oiled leather. "Attention. Announcement is. Lord Jansz joins for lunch."

"I bid you welcome," said Belladonna in a precise manner as far from her wind-chime laugh as the moon is from the sun.

"Please . . ."

". . . forgive . . ."

". . . the . . ."

". . . unusual . . ."

". . . social . . ."

". . . arrangements." The AB-clones' bird-like voices dovetailed in precise sequence.

"All newcomers are examined . . ." Graohl rumbled threateningly.

". . . before being invited to trade," Roahr added,

shifting on her perch and clasping her hands across her scaled belly.

Crichton watched three sets of lustrous wings and two intricately patterned starfishlike limbs make identical movements—insofar as their anatomy would allow.

Zhaan nodded, ever the diplomat. "We understand there are protocols involved."

"I'm afraid it's far more than protocol," said Belladonna.

"It's a matter of security," rumbled Graohl.

"As Trader-Prime to the Nomad Flotilla," continued Roahr in sepulchral tones.

"I have many enemies." Graohl added firmly.

"And . . ."

". . . thus . . ."

". . . also . . ."

". . . a . . ."

". . . pardonable . . ."

". . . indulgence . . ."

". . . in . . ."

". . . personal . . ."

". . . safety . . ."

". . . precautions," whistled the AB-clones in conclusion.

Crichton, like D'Argo and Chiana, found his gaze passing rapidly from one speaker to the next, as individual members of the Compound carried on Jansz's conversation. Only Albedo seemed content—if that was a word you could apply to a slowly spinning crystal cube—to observe.

Zhaan alone seemed unfazed by the conversation.

"When may we expect to be able to discuss our needs?"

Belladonna delicately wiped her mouth with a napkin. Five other limbs imitated the gesture. "I have yet to satisfy myself of your intentions."

Crichton found himself wondering what kind of a creature Jansz was. Why did he have to maintain this shield between him and the rest of the cosmos? Since leaving Earth, Crichton had encountered any number of alien species with unusual characteristics. Perhaps Jansz fell into the all-brain-and-no-brawn category. Crichton imagined a cold intellect capable of running something the size of the Nomad Flotilla housed in a body perhaps as small and fragile as a hermit crab. Actually that wasn't such a bad analogy. Hermit crabs looked at the world from inside a shell, or a shoe or whatever bit of flotsam they happened to find, that was the right size when they abandoned their old home. Crichton shivered abruptly. It wasn't such a big leap from listening to Jansz observing the world through the senses of his Compound to wondering whether the trader could use other bodies for his needs, perhaps involuntarily.

And with this thought Crichton had, finally, had enough. "Look, let's cut to the chase," he said. "I've had enough of this crap and I'm sure everyone else has as well. You want something from this meeting or you wouldn't have invited us here. I've been sizing you up, Jansz, and I think I know what you want. You want the thrill of the chase. You want to wind us up, watch us dance. Oh, you'll trade eventually . . . when you're ready. That's not good enough for us. See, I don't care if you trust us, I don't care if I trust you. A trade is not based on trust. It's business. You know it. I know it. There's something we need. We've told you what it is. Trade for it or we'll leave. Moya will die and you'll lose any potential for entertainment this situation might have."

"One . . ."

". . . prefers . . ."

". . . the . . ."

". . . word . . ."

". . . fulfillment . . ."

". . . but . . ."

". . . that . . ."

". . . aside . . ."

". . . one . . ."

". . . concedes . . ."

". . . your . . ."

". . . point . . ."

Now we're cruising, thought Crichton, feeling relieved. His companions were staring at him with a mixture of astonishment and anger. "And by the way, Jansz, you can quit showing off with the shop dummy routine. It gives me whiplash. You can get in here in person and rap with the crew. Or we walk. And don't worry—we don't care what you look like. Slug, snail, spider . . . you don't have anything to fear from us."

Crichton folded his arms and waited. Abruptly, the Compound dissolved—burst, almost, like a bubble— and the dining room was full of individuals again.

Belladonna broke the shocked silence. "Well, John Crichton, I must confess to being a little startled. Don't get me wrong, I admire a firm mind. But this takes the concept into previously uncharted territory."

"Call it a way of life." Crichton reached for his fork and speared a morsel of food.

"IF YOU WISH."

Crichton almost jumped out of his skin. The voice was thunderous.

Crichton looked up—slowly.

The creature towering over him stood about four meters at the shoulder. The head was . . . that is, the face was . . . well, the word "face" was something of a misnomer. Imagine a sheet of six-inch shark's teeth wrapped around the skull of a Kodiak bear. An angry Kodiak. With four mouths. Mouths that housed tongues like coils of barbed wire. Eyes like nests of gleaming beetles. Arms built of layer upon layer of hard muscle interleaved with what looked like skin-steel, and topped with a single ridge of diamond-hard plates that resembled the spine of a stegosaurus.

It could only be Jansz. Crichton whistled. *There goes the hermit crab theory. And then some.*

Vurid stood on five quivering legs and announced. "Lord Jansz is."

"Thank you, Vurid. Clearly our guests have noticed that one has joined them."

"Yeah, well, you're a bit hard to miss, you know," quipped Crichton, regaining his composure.

"Oh? Not a slug, or a snail, or a spider?"

"Uh . . . actually . . . no." Crichton remembered to swallow.

"Well, one is very pleased to hear it. It's an unforgiving universe, after all, and one so hates to be misunderstood."

"Indeed." Zhaan smiled ingratiatingly.

Crichton shrugged. *How was I to know?*

"So." Jansz seated himself, with considerable grace for one so large, at the empty place. "Negotiations have commenced. And it seems one has a worthy opponent in the Moya party."

Crichton frowned, thought for a moment, then stood up. "Nah, you're just rubbing my rhubarb." To the others, he added, "Come on, we're outta here."

"Leaving so soon?" Jansz's silky solo voice hinted at threat.

"It's a big galaxy. We'll take our chances."

Abruptly Jansz rose. Without a sound he dismissed the Compound. Only Jansz, Vurid and Albedo Point Zero Eight remained; the alum cube rotated slowly upon its pedestal. The platters ascended on their chains into the serving hatches set into the ceiling. Lunch was over.

"And now we may pay respectful attention to one another's needs. Conditions for trade are simple," Jansz continued. "By giving you what you want I will be saving not one life but many. Therefore, you must each trade separately. Agree to this and the matter will be treated as a single exchange."

"And if we don't?" demanded D'Argo.

"You may—as you say—take your chances elsewhere."

Zhaan spoke for the crew after a brief whispered conference.

"We agree," she said. "We'll trade separately."

"Good. Then we'll begin with . . ." Jansz's huge skull moved with controlled power as he scanned the visitors with keen eyes. "You." The eyes fastened on Chiana. "The individual known, if one recalls accurately, as Chiana. What will you trade for your life?"

"Anything that I can steal for you."

Jansz laughed, all of his voices rumbling together in discordant amusement. "This trade is acceptable."

He turned to D'Argo. "Luxan warrior, what is your life worth?"

"My life is worth nothing."

"What, then, do you have to trade?"

"What do I have to trade?" D'Argo's voice was bitter. "I have nothing to trade. I have lost everything— my wife and child—everything most precious to me."

Jansz's head tilted to one side, considering. "You have friends?"

"I do."

"Then you could trade one of your friends. For your life."

D'Argo sprang to his feet, fists clenched, murder in his eyes. Jansz did not flinch. Seated, he was still eye-to-eye with the furious Luxan.

"You would do well to consider what you ask," D'Argo spat. "I would never trade a friend for my life."

"Even to see your child again?"

D'Argo took a step closer to Jansz. Chiana scrambled quickly aside, while Crichton, Aeryn, and Zhaan stayed where they were. Jansz had no idea of the powder keg he was close to igniting.

"Easy, big guy," Crichton urged. "He doesn't want you to betray us. He just wants to play with your head."

"Then I would suggest he has already won more than a fair trade."

"Right. Good. So sit down, OK? We could all still come out of this alive."

D'Argo sat, slowly, never taking his eyes off Jansz.

Jansz considered. "A brief trade, but . . . yes. Your emotional turmoil was enjoyable. And your guilt, confusion, anger, all these have now been digitized for resale. They will fetch a handsome profit. This trade is acceptable."

Jansz glanced at Albedo Point Zero Eight, who glided from the room, still spinning gently.

D'Argo sat, seething at the way he had been manipulated.

Zhaan met Jansz's gaze calmly, waiting, face composed, tranquil. Crichton wondered how hard it was to maintain that degree of control. Zhaan seemed about to speak when Aeryn interrupted, speaking directly to Jansz herself. "You've been very direct about what you want from us. But what can you offer in return?"

Jansz did not turn. Apparently those crawling-beetle eyes saw everything—and everyone. "One offers what you want. A cure."

"And that is?"

"Relatively simple. Your starship is a female Leviathan. From observations taken as you approached it is clear she has given birth. It's safe to assume she is fertile."

"I don't see what relevance that information has."

"The explanation is simple. Your starship will provide her own cure . . . in part, at least. One egg will be required—oh, not for trade, you understand, no. The procreation process differs little from species to species. All eggs are formed of undifferentiated cells. At some point during gestation chemical triggers tell those cells to differentiate—to grow into organs, bone, brain tissue, skin, eyes, hair, and so forth. One of the Leviathan's eggs will provide the undifferentiated cells. I will supply the chemical triggers necessary to allow a carefully positioned bolus of undifferentiated cells to regrow the organ that has been destroyed. Once injected, Moya will be able to stabilize her own hormonal balance."

Zhaan frowned. "Where will the chemical triggers come from?"

"That depends. I have access to various sources: animals culled from non-high-tech worlds that have no other use. One such was recently acquired from an unstable world. It would otherwise have died. Now it will perform a valuable purpose. One's fleet has been searching for other such unstable worlds. They provide a rich bounty to those with the power to exploit them. "As you already know, my apothecary is famous."

Crichton cleared his throat. "You know, I don't want to throw a damp squid here, but do we even know Moya will allow the egg to be removed?"

Aeryn frowned. "She hardly has a choice. If she dies, her eggs die as well."

"It's a discussion we can leave for later," Zhaan commented.

"One disagrees," Jansz countered. "The remaining undifferentiated cells are the price one demands from Moya to save her life."

D'Argo's breath hissed from between his teeth. The conversation was laying bare a lot of nerves.

Crichton shot D'Argo a glance that said, "Later, big guy." To Jansz he said aloud, "OK, looks like you got your deal."

Jansz's attention remained focused on Zhaan. "And what will you trade for your life?"

"I will trade sex for my life—and for Moya's life. At a time and place of your choosing."

Crichton struggled to retain control.

Zhaan continued, "I am a Tenth-level Pa'u, well versed in bodily control. I learned Iolantric pollination at the hands of three masters. It is my best offer."

Jansz considered—briefly. "Agreed. The Compound will consummate this trade before you leave. Privately, of course. The nature of your individuality is understood."

"As you wish."

Jansz now regarded Aeryn. His compound eyes focused on the darkly beautiful Sebacean.

With characteristic directness, Aeryn did not allow the Trader-Prime to speak first. "I'll trade my Peacekeeper identity. I have a credit chip. A passport. ID bracelets. DNA fingerprint. You can have them all. I'm sure they'll be worth a great deal on the black market."

"We know you have been banished. Any attempt to utilize your identity would be immediately recognized."

"It's all I have."

"Do you have any currency?"

"No."

"Perhaps I could hire your services as a troubleshooter."

"As what? An assassin? An enforcer? I don't think so."

"Then we do not, regretfully, have a deal."

"Wait, wait up," Crichton interrupted suddenly. "I'll trade for Aeryn."

Jansz's head rocked thoughtfully. "Interesting. Selfless. A sacrifice of personal wealth for another who is poor. A notion linked to individuality, of course, and an interesting one. What will you trade, John Crichton?"

"You look like a—trader—who can appreciate art."

"Indeed. One considers oneself a connoisseur."

"Yeah, well, consider this. I can trade art that no one, and I mean no one in your entire galaxy has ever seen or heard before. Classical work that in my culture would buy entire countries. A cultural inheritance that would be unique in the experience of everyone you know and anyone you are ever likely to meet, barring the odd freak wormhole."

"I am intrigued, though I sense exaggeration on your part."

"Well, let me put it to you like this: you don't need to know how much this art is worth—only what it is worth to you. And you'll have a corner on the market, won't you? You'll be the sole supplier."

"You may continue."

"First agree that you'll let me trade for Aeryn."

"Agreed. Proceed."

"Alright. You like music?"

"Very much. A classical art form. Next to mathematics and emotional synthesis, music is the highest form of creative expression."

"Great." Crichton cheered inwardly. "You ever heard of ZZ Top?"

Jansz salivated; a single drop of saliva cut a smoking track in his steel collar.

"What about Elvis? The Carpenters? Abba? The Beach Boys?"

"You have all these pieces to trade?"

"I've got many . . . pieces."

"And you would be willing to trade?"

"All of them."

"Then we have a deal."

"Great, great. Now if we can just—"

"A moment. Negotiations are not yet concluded."

"Huh?"

Crichton glanced around the dining room. Hadn't everyone traded? He and Aeryn, Zhaan, D'Argo, Chiana . . . hold it. What's wrong with this picture? Crichton rose angrily. "Where the hell is Rygel?"

Jansz's ship was much more than a simple vehicle. It was a space-going town—almost a city. Measuring nine kilometers across its beam and fifteen kilometers from stem to stern, it was even bigger than Moya.

The ship was laid out like a city, with buildings and parks spread out beneath clear elongated canopies, which allowed natural sunlight to enter the living environments while blocking ultraviolet rays and other dangerous radiation. The domes were arranged on the inner surface of a ring-habitat that, rotated gently to that Coriolis force, created a gravity of about .75g at the surface. Water flowed in artistic ripples at this gravity; and walking was amusing—if a little on the wild side.

The domes—six in all—were longer than they were wide. Three enclosed spaces designated for living, working, and trading, and three enclosed hydroponics areas where greenery from fifty different worlds traded sunlight and recycled waste for breathable air. The domes were separated by six fluted oval columns that curved up from wide bases and narrowed to meet at a central hub, where the engines and navigation control centers were located.

The design was old—it had even been postulated on

Earth—but in this case Jansz had had the ship retrofitted with the most modern engines, navigational equipment, and amenities that legitimate trade (and a little rude piracy on the side) could provide.

Jansz's crew stayed with the trader not just because he provided a steady income, but also because, when all was said and done, he treated the thousands of people who worked for him relatively well. The crew delighted in spreading the myth of Jansz as a ruthless and violent entity amongst the galaxy because that gave him an advantage in matters of trade—something that, ultimately, benefited them as well.

Nevertheless, daily life on the ship was fairly routine, involving nearly five thousand crew and twice that many traders moving to and fro amongst the ever-changing ships of the flotilla on a daily basis. Security was minimal—because everyone was armed. Jansz did not care about enforcing any laws. Why should he spend the money when traders were quite capable of enforcing the law themselves? If any one merchant became too powerful or rich, Jansz simply enforced a 90 percent supertax at gunpoint, bankrupting the merchant in question and spreading the newly acquired profit amongst the private security force he hired to do the job. This aside, anyone could make a reasonable profit under Jansz's protection.

On any one day, then, the crowded marketplaces, stretching over a curving area equal to about the size of a small town, were both efficient and rowdy; businesslike and characterized by drunken bawdiness.

In many ways this setup called to mind the medieval cultures on many inhabited worlds throughout the galaxy. Jansz was a feudal lord and exacted a tax for every entry into and departure from his marketplace; every rented accommodation, every bottle of air, every liter of water, every ounce of food and fuel sold in his space. He rarely bought stock himself—he had no need of trade because his taxes were so efficient. Thus he reserved for himself the pleasure of a trade now and again—but this took the form of a dalliance, almost; a pleasure akin to a hobby.

Though his roots were in piracy, Jansz had little need of piracy now. He was an older, wiser, and more mature being than he had been during his impetuous youth. Now structure and trade, carefully controlled and actively encouraged with lotteries and prizes for amusing contests, was a far more lucrative way to turn a profit than looting and pillaging.

Truth be known, Jansz was well on the way to becoming one of the richest beings in the Uncharted Territories. Of course, this was not entirely to his advantage. Wealth brought autonomy and in the wider political circles of the galaxy that was often interpreted as a threat. There were species who had long kept a careful eye, or antennae, on Jansz, and it was often that pressure was brought to bear on intersystem councils to curb the Trader-Prime's activity in a manner similar, though more violent, to that by which he enforced the law in his own marketplace.

Indeed, there were many freelance mercenary forces for hire in the cold reaches of space. Many to whom the thought of looting and piracy (or to give it its proper term, government-sanctioned economic cull-ing) was attractive. But this was a life Jansz had led before, and so far he'd had no problem repelling any minor incursions by small forces that managed to keep track of his nomad existence.

Of course, this was a process that could not be maintained forever. No security force is perfect, nor any economic structure. As a matter of historical fact, luck had nearly always played some kind of role in trade throughout the centuries in hundreds of civilizations across the galaxy.

And Jansz was soon to discover that luck—in the form of a certain small Hynerian named Rygel—had just taken a not entirely insignificant hand in the running of his affairs.

The main thoroughfare of Trade Dome One was practically a boulevard. Broad and long, the thoroughfare was half-cylindrical, with curved plexalloy shopfronts spaced at regular intervals. Overhead a transparent dome showed the flaming mass of a spiral galaxy that backlit half of the trader fleet. Off to one side, drifting slowly from view as the fleet moved on, was the close mass of the blue supergiant star. Broad-leafed palms with spiky branches erupted joyfully from marbled cubes set into the walls and floor. Life forms of many different species crowded the space, jostling for position and trading in loud voices. Rygel found that the endless barks, squeals, and hissing clicks made him faintly nauseous. And since the assassination attempt hundreds of cycles ago, he wasn't entirely comfortable in crowds. Cutting the ribbonworm on a new center for Hynerian trade and industry was one thing . . . being shot at by a frelling maniac with a pocket-singularity-launcher was quite another. Fortunately, his security staff had been alert and that was the end of the pathetic trog. No civilians were harmed and there had been almost no blood to clear up.

Rygel shivered at the memory. It had all happened a long time ago, shortly after his coronation, and was generally something he preferred not to think about. Particularly not now. Since the coup, and his one hundred and thirty cycles of incarceration, Rygel had learned how to take great pleasure from the smallest of achievements. Right now he was exceptionally pleased with himself.

Escaping the lunch had been easy. The platters had been rising and falling continually on their chains as they were emptied and refilled with food. Each time his platter had been replaced, Rygel had urged his ThroneSled a little nearer the ceiling. Once above eye-height, it had been easy to slip from the dining room unobserved. It didn't matter what world you came from, how your brain worked or whether you were an individual or part of a gestalt. The cleverest person in the universe never looked up when they were eating. Or away when arguing.

Rygel allowed himself a smug chuckle. He had always counted himself among the cleverest of his people—how else could he have become such a popular Dominar?—and any opportunity to display that cleverness gave a him a warm tingling feeling from his leathery ears to his hairy toes. On good days, just being himself was enough to call a healthy glow to his cheeks and the pleasant aroma of hydrogen sulphide to his skin. Of course, most days weren't good days, and hadn't been for some time. But that would change. As soon as he returned to Hyneria and dispensed the punishment that the frelling Bishan so richly deserved. It had been a long time since there had been a public execution on Hyneria. Then again, treason was the most terrible of crimes—particularly when one happened to be on the receiving end of it—reason enough to dig a new drowning pit.

Rygel found himself shivering. It really was altogether too easy to become a victim of one's own nightmares and fantasies. With an effort, he focused on the here and now, edging his ThroneSled half a meter higher in order to drift over the heads of the crowd.

His mouth curled in a slippery-lipped smile.

No one would ever find him in this crowd.

Then again, it was also boring. The shops, the people, the hype, the inconsequential mundanity of it all. As boring as the conversation he had been so glad to escape.

Rygel sighed. His life had once been rich and satisfying. Born to the royal family of Hyneria, one of the greatest empires in the galaxy, all Rygel had known from the moment his eyes opened and cool grey-green Hynerian daylight had first bathed his face had been the diligent attention that maids, butlers, dressers, chefs, and myriad other servants paid his every whim. He was their destiny. The royal blood of generations flowed through his veins, pulsed in his heart. He was Hyneria of Hyneria. The Dominar-To-Be. And woe betide anyone who did not make it their life's business to know it.

His youth had been spent playing the games that Hynerians of royal blood had played forever . . . Taunt the Butler, Flaunt the Power, Dungeons and Damsels. As a child, he had been intelligent, articulate and imaginative . . . but also selfish, acquisitive, and, at times, downright idiotic.

In other words, Rygel now realized, exactly like he was now!

Well, of course, that was to be expected, wasn't it?
It was drummed into him by every member of his family, at every possible moment, what a special child he
was. The laity worshipped him as a god among gods;
his servants fulfilled his every whim; his family looked
upon him with eyes that could see no wrong. And yet
to Rygel XVI, the word "special" quickly came to
mean rigid protocol, stifled interests, endless lectures
on social etiquette, political intrigue, and the dangers
of close friendships.

He was special, oh, yes. He was also bored, lonely,
fearful, and distrustful. He was afraid of the dark and
of quiet places; comfortable only in the moon-pool,
the centerpiece of the Palace of Suns, the Summer
Palace built in the verdant southern hemisphere by
Dominar Rygel IX, more than a thousand cycles before. He did not know happiness nor yet, he had since
realized with much regret, did he miss the feeling—for
several cycles anyway.

The summer of his twenty-ninth birthday. That was
when it had all changed. That was when he had met
Nyaella. That was when he had first known love.

Oh, he had known friendships, minor courtships, the
curious adoration of purchased courtesans, and the
usual political maneuvring among the royal family
lines. But this was no moon-feeling, no shallow whiff
of hydrogen sulphide upon the skin. This was full-
blown sun-feeling. His skin sweated pure hydrocarbon
for a week, flushing the baby-fat away and leaving him
lean and muscled beneath the mottled, granular skin of
youth. His leathery ears stood proud on his regal head,
his skin flushed blue with interest at the slightest
provocation, and he blossomed in height, finally top-

ping out at an amazing sixty centimeters, an impressive height and one that had not been officially recorded among the royal family since the heady days of Rygel the Great, founder of the great Hynerian Dynasty, several thousand cycles before.

Noonspurner, Grand Vizier to Rygel's father, was often heard to despair about the future of the royal line. Visitors to the Palace were frequently to overhear this smooth, ancient creature issue forth upon the dangers of love, the follies of youth, and the tribulations of those responsible for their education and protection.

"Love is it? Love? He'll be the undoing of the dynasty. Why only last sun, at the moon-pool, I saw him and that cousin of his holding hands. I tell you, it's positively dangerous. Love indeed! More important, I say, to think of alliances, of the future. But who listens to me? Certainly not Rygel the New. He thinks not of tomorrow, only now."

But Rygel did not need to listen to the court gossip, the kitchen scuttlebutt. Lies and exaggeration and intrigue meant nothing to him. He knew the matter for which wagging tongues and rolling eyes numbering in the hundreds found so much favor. He knew the truth. Her name was Nyaella Skitrovex.

Rygel, of course, knew her as Joy, as Excitement, as Laughter, as Companionship, and as Freedom; in short, as all the things a rigidly political birth from royal lineage had denied him for the whole of his life thus far.

The Lady Nyaella Skitrovex was Rygel's second cousin and the loveliest of all the royals. Rygel was handsome and intelligent. A relationship between them was forbidden. Was it any wonder they fell in love?

Nyaella Skitrovex was two suns older than Rygel. Graced with a perfect, pear-shaped figure and gloriously mottled skin, her royal lineage was unmistakable. The royal portraitists liked painting no one as much as Nyaella. Her eyes, like deep pools, were the color of teaweed and her breath the rich scent of summer. Her posture neatly rounded, her limbs the stubby icon of Hynerian perfection, the Royal Documentors had no need to employ their carefully designed (and concealed) ArtWare filters to improve her looks. Not only this, but Nyaella quickly developed a passion for Hynerian rights, education, and social improvement that easily lifted her head and shoulders above the average hands-off politician.

Many Hynerians believed that she was just the princess the empire needed. Before securing his father's approval, the daring couple rashly revealed their secret romance to an adoring public. Not one to admit his son had acted without his consent, Rygel XV celebrated the engagement with days of feasting and a display of fireworks that lit up the night sky for hours.

Rygel and Nyaella were perfect together. Which, of course, sent six dozen viziers into a shudder of panic; hundreds of court officials scuttling for political cover, further thousands into a social feeding frenzy and his mother, the Dominae, into a perfect slither of unparalleled delight.

Only his father was not impressed. But then, when had his father ever been impressed by anything he had chosen to do? The old Dominar had taken him aside one evening—a rare occurrence and one that made Rygel feel unaccountable disquiet—for a walk along the ramparts of the family home, the hereditary seat of Hynerian power.

The Summer Palace had been built high upon the ramparts of a mountain range overlooking the steeply shelving wine-ponds of the southern continent. The night was warm and fragrant with the heady scent of teaweed, a vital component in the fermentation of the best Hynerian vintage. Music drifted across the palace walls, the gypsy ragas twining sinuously as the many flaming torches held by the thousands of wine-treaders walking the millions of steps necessary to ensure a small portion of Hynerian future prosperity. A hundred voices raised themselves in counterpoint to the music, leading the pattern of treading, accompanied by the excited cries and splashes of children, the whole a mute whisper borne upon a warm breeze and carried far across the moonlit night.

Rygel listened to the voices and each one seemed to be the voice of one of the myriad stars that, reflected densely in the polished marble walls, gave the Palace of Suns its name.

Rygel XV was old, skin smooth as his voice, translucent with age, devoid of any real tactile surfaces, and almost completely white. Under the bone-pale moon he appeared ghostly, a specter of the royal line. The fact was that it had been so many cycles since they had met for any length of time that his son could not remember how old the Dominar actually looked in the hot light of day. Rygel found himself wondering how much of his father's appearance was due simply to the moonlight bleaching out any color that may have been visible in his skin, and how much was actually due to age.

To see him at his true height, without the security and

comfort of his ThroneSled, was even more disturbing.

"Your mother is very pleased with your choice of life-partner." The old Dominar's voice was smooth, lacking the characteristic gurgle of youth, the considered liquidity of middle-age.

"I am glad, Father. Many are pleased."

"And does it seem also that there are those who are *dis*pleased by your match?"

The young Rygel felt a momentary shudder. "I don't know what you mean, Father."

The old Dominar flashed Rygel an angry look. "Then tell me, have your education and training been entirely wasted?"

"I . . ." Rygel stammered before his father's rage. But then the Old Dominar softened his voice.

"My son, you have many gifts. All these tools a Dominar must know how to use, if he is to survive, and serve. You may think that everything you want will be yours for the asking. And much will be. But consider also what position you hold within this Empire. You and I, my son, we are the Empire. I am fading now, but you are its bright tomorrow. With this position comes certain responsibilities. Certain duties."

Rygel felt his skin flush a shade warmer than could be accounted for by the warmth of the evening. "You don't want me to marry her, do you?"

"What you or I want is not at issue here. I want you to be happy. I want you to be a good Dominar for our people. You want to be with Nyaella. You want to enjoy life. These things may not be . . . *convenient*."

"I overheard Noonspurner say the same thing only this afternoon to some visiting dignitaries from Archaeleon. What does it mean, Father? Am I not allowed to love, to think for myself? Am I to be considered *inconvenient* if I do?"

"A Dominar must never be eclipsed by his own shadow."

"I don't understand."

"A Dominar rules. Not his queen, not his lover. It's fine that Nyaella is beautiful and intelligent. But she is also popular. As queen, her popularity will bring her power. This is dangerous. There must be no rival for the love of the people. No rival for the Dominar. It is a hard lesson, but one you must learn, or there may be no Empire to rule."

"Father, why are you doing this?"

"Because I love the Empire. And because I love you."

"And which do you love more?"

"You are the same thing. My son, the Empire."

Rygel XV drew himself up to his full height, and looked up at the youth who would carry his genes into the future. "When a Dominar stands in the hot light of day he must cast no shadow."

Even now the memory of his father's words made Rygel shudder. He remembered how his stomach had churned and his skin grew clammy when he realized what would happen to Nyaella if he didn't do as his father wished.

"But I love Nyaella. And she loves me. You can't . . ."

". . . kill her?" His father's voice was cold. "No . . . but she could become ill, be injured in an accident . . . perhaps even fatally or . . ."

Rygel bit his lip so hard blood flowed—the scar would stay with him always.

He leaned on the ramparts, clutching his chest,

gasping for breath. The wine-making ragas still gave voice to the night, but now it was no lovely melody but a discordant howl that threatened to deafen him. His heart beat wildly in his chest and the blood pounded in his ears. He drew a shuddering breath and struggled to compose himself.

"What will happen to Nyaella if I do not see her again?"

His father looked relieved. "No harm will come to her."

Rygel touched a stubby finger to his lip, studied the blood that adhered to his granular skin. Royal blood. Had he ever thought it would bring him such pain? "Tomorrow I will tell Nyaella our engagement is over."

"I think it best . . . if you did not see her. It will be less painful in the long run."

"Your wish, Father, is mine to obey."

But even as his lips framed the words, Rygel knew that he was lying.

Rygel was brought unceremoniously back to the present when a particularly tall alien, whom he recognized as a female Thrantillil, brushed her broad, ribbed skull against the underside of his ThroneSled. "Watch where you're going," she snarled. Rygel quickly moved aside—Thrantillil, especially the females, were well known for their nasty tempers, and he wanted to avoid any confrontation.

The crowd closed around him and he felt a brief moment of fear. Being surrounded by people had never been a problem for the Dominar before he was deposed and imprisoned, but since his escape each day brought unforeseen problems. His body seemed to delight in reacting to any new situation, no matter how ordinary, as if it were life-threatening.

Like this situation, for instance. How could a toothache put them all in such peril? Ridiculous! Like all Hynerians, Rygel had not developed teeth for nearly six cycles, but—oh!—what teeth they were. He'd had them for hundreds of cycles already and they only showed the most minor signs of wear. And as for infection? Also, ridiculous! Unheard of! What, Rygel wondered, were Crichton's teeth made of anyway that one actually would be rotting in his mouth? It really must be terrible to be a human.

The crowd was becoming more dense, and Rygel was finding the close press of bodies distasteful. At one time, when the bodies were his own loyal subjects, it was thrilling. But this was different. No one cared about him, no one respected his personal space, no one even noticed him. For Rygel, the time spent on Moya had been an unrelenting reminder that while he was a very important someone on his home world, out here in the Uncharted Territories he was just another curious alien, a small fish in a very big pond.

A small, lonely fish.

Rygel sometimes felt foolish for indulging in dreams of home. But what could he do? He hadn't seen another Hynerian for more than three hundred cycles, and though he was selfish and spoiled, he also was devoted to his people. As a youth, he had often wondered how it would be to sneak away from the Palace of Suns and join in the wine-stamping rituals, to become lost in the ragas, the dancing, the delightful company of strangers who had no idea of who he was.

What Rygel missed more than anything was companionship.

Friendship.

Understanding.

Sympathy.

Sex.

Rygel shuddered. In this press of alien bodies of every age and species, he felt more alone than ever, more alienated, more—

Wait.

Rygel's ThroneSled hovered in midair, causing a minor obstruction of traffic and some loud complaints.

Wait . . .

Rygel circled slowly over the jostling crowd.

Something . . .

Something familiar . . .

The ThroneSled sped along a narrow side-corridor. The shop-fronts here had given way to cloth-fronted stalls, crammed even closer together with a dense mass of hawkers, traders, and the idle curious.

Smells exploded around him: foods, spices, herbs, incense, and pots of strange bubbling liquids . . .

But over all this, a more pervasive scent.

There!

That scent! It was—

A slight moan escaped from Rygel's throat.

Another Hynerian.

A *female.*

Could he be dreaming? Oh, land of his mothers, not another desperate delusion, a mistake that would keep him trembling with embarrassment in his quarters for weeks.

Rygel urged his ThroneSled above the press of bodies, scooting speedily along the passageway, avoiding hanging baskets of fruit and vegetation. The scent drew him on, captive, body and soul, thought gone, erased in the desperate realization of precisely how lonely he really was.

The passageway ended at a crossroads with several different paths. Rygel sniffed the air. The scent seemed fainter. Had he imagined it? A combination of exotic fruits and seeds? Perhaps the bubbling liquid . . . ?

No.

There!

Rygel chose a path to the right.

The scent grew stronger.

A shaft opened into a circular chamber lit by hundreds of red candles. The walls were hung with tapestries. Rygel blinked. The red end of the spectrum had always been something of a mystery to his species.

The sole occupant reclined upon a circular bed piled with pillows of bendigan fire silk. A golden chain, fastened to a collar around her neck, was bolted to a post.

The Hynerienne sat up.

"Hello, darling," said Nyaella Skitrovex.

For a moment Rygel could only stare, openmouthed. "What . . . ?" he began, stupidly. "How . . . ?"

Nyaella's composure crumpled, her eyes filled with tears, her voice broke. "I've dreamed of this day, but I never . . . I mean, I did dream but . . ."

She slipped off the bed, chains clinking quietly, then made a formal bow of obeisance—a display of respect that Rygel had almost despaired of ever seeing again. Her voice firmed. "How utterly exquisite to see you after all this time."

He was about to speak when a section of wall slid open. And he heard an eerie, but familiar, sound. Four aliens of different species were standing motionless in an alcove. They were all breathing in perfect time.

Nyaella stretched out on the bed. "Rygel, allow me to introduce Trader-Prime Jansz." Shifting her attention to the Compound, she added, "Darling, this is Rygel XVI, Dominar of the . . ."

". . . Hynerian Empire. I know. We've met." Four voices spoke as one. "Well, Rygel, one trusts that you have enjoyed your exploration of one's humble world."

"Yes. Indeed." Rygel felt like a child caught with his fingers in the candy jar. "It's very . . . *hrumph*—very interesting."

"Of course, it can in no way compare with the splendor of your own domain . . . nonetheless, it is one I am very comfortable in."

"I'm . . . I'm glad." *Where was this going? What was Nyaella doing on Jansz's ship? And in chains? Why was she a prisoner? Was she a hostage? For ransom? Was his treacherous cousin Bishan, who had stolen his throne, involved in some way?*

Jansz's Compound spoke again. "While you have been exploring, one has reached an agreement to supply a cure for Moya. The last component of the agreement is a trade with yourself. By saving Moya's life, one will obviously save each of her crew as well. So tell me, Rygel XVI of Hyneria, what is your life worth?"

Rygel felt his ears burn. The skin on his stubby forearms smoothed. His cheeks flushed with anger.

"Your arrogance is beyond comprehension. You keep a member of the Royal Family of Hyneria in chains and ask what I would trade for my life?"

The Compound's eyes tracked Rygel carefully as he drew himself up to his full height of sixty centimeters. "I will not trade for my life or anyone's while such contempt is shown towards a member of my family! I will, however," and here his voice assumed a threatening tone his father would have been proud of, "promise you that if you do not give us what we want immediately, and release the Lady Nyaella Skitrovex, I will use every method at my disposal to ensure your slow and painful death!"

Jansz's response came quickly.

"I have enjoyed meeting you and the rest of the Moya party. It is regrettable that you have prevented a bargain from being struck. I wish you well in your search for a cure for your ship. The Compound will escort you back to your vessel. This meeting is over."

Dumbly, Rygel was led from the chamber. Just before the shaft closed, he glanced back to see a frightened but hopeful smile from Nyaella. She had once believed in him, and he had betrayed her.

Now, through sheer stupidity, he had betrayed her again.

CHAPTER 4

Back on Moya, Crichton had some choice words for the ex-Dominar. "Hey, Sparky, wanna let me in on your little secret?" His voice, already sharp with anger, took on a razor's edge of sarcasm. "I mean, looky here, Big Green's found a great new game to play. It's called 'How to get your buddies killed'! You want to tell me what the rules are, your Highness? Screw your friends over at the first sniff of a good lay? Is that it?

Jeez, Rygel, what the hell do you think you're playing at?"

Rygel clung with both hands to the edge of his ThroneSled. He was surrounded by a circle of furious people. Their anger washed against him, battered him this way and that like a moonswept tide. He glanced from one pair of angry eyes to another, the ThroneSled bobbing as he sought some way to escape them. There was none. He was forced to endure their unfair and un-relenting accusations.

". . . you trying to get us killed?"

". . . always thinking of yourself!?"

". . . dying ship not enough for you, huh? Got to shaft your friends as well?"

". . . a brain that small is clearly incapable of under-standing the concept of friendship, let alone loyalty!"

". . . we'll be lucky to get out of this in one piece!"

". . . pray we do not survive. If we do I will kill you myself. Your death will be slow as befits a fool. Slow and painful."

Rygel found himself spinning in circles. Not since his father's assassination had he felt so alone, so vul-nerable. "I . . ." his voice was unsteady. He tried to inject a measure of firmness into it, the sound of au-thority that a Dominar should project to his people. It had been too long. He couldn't do it. It was all too much! Why couldn't they just shut up and leave him alone!

But, as usual, Rygel overcame his feelings of guilt and shame and allowed his anger to attain full bloom.

"I think you've made your feelings clear," Rygel began in his most pompous and patronizing tone. "Now, could I please have *your* attention? There are some things I wish to say. First, you are all here by *my* sufferance. It was my intelligence and skill that engi-neered Moya's escape from the frelling Peacekeepers and, therefore, it should be clear that each and every one of *you* owes *me* your life!"

Silence. Only Rygel could twist the situation around like that.

"Second, in case it has escaped your notice, I am a Dominar, and wish to be treated like one!"

Rygel urged his ThroneSled above their heads. Let them look up at him. The time for making excuses for stupid people was over. He was wound up now. There was no stopping this tirade.

"Why am I not surprised that even simple respect for a travelling companion seems beyond you? No, don't bother to answer. You're clearly incapable of the slightest empathy. It's why you're always arguing. But let me tell you this. I'm tired, very, very tired, of constantly having to make allowances for your ignorance and selfishness. Not one of you has the slightest idea how to comport yourself in public or show the most basic level of respect to anyone who doesn't agree with your own needs. Not one of you has the ability to place yourself in another's position, to even try to understand why he might choose to do the things he does. All you ever think about is *me me me!* Well, think about this: I was old when your great-grandparents were barely conceived and I have lived a life beyond your capacity to imagine."

Rygel found his breath coming faster as the memories caused his heart to beat wildly in his chest. "I have held the lives of billions in my hands. Judged the fate of worlds. I have been a politician, a leader, and a martyr. I have been betrayed by a queen and I have held a dying Dominar in my arms, swearing with all my heart to wear his mantle with pride and respect and humility even as his blood dried on my skin. I have heard my name sung in hymns by six hundred billion voices. All this and more have I done in the name of my empire, my people. And now you, you who would be less than teaweeders on my world, you presume to treat me in this intolerable and ignorant manner! *I won't have it, do you hear? I won't!"*

Rygel struggled to regain his breath. "I have my reasons for doing what I did, saying what I did. You cannot possibly understand. Nyaella Skitrovex is of the royal blood line of Hyneria. A single minute of her life is worth a thousand of your lives, ten thousand such ships as Moya. She is worth worlds to me. You are not even worthy of my notice."

"We understand your feelings, Rygel," said Zhaan, "but we cannot let you sacrifice Moya. You must change your request. You must agree to trade with Jansz for a cure for Moya. Or we will all die."

Rygel did not hesitate. His voice was firm.

"The only trade I will make is for Nyaella."

"Then we have no choice."

Five pairs of hands grabbed Rygel, lifted him from his ThroneSled, and bore him from the bridge.

For a brief time, Rygel had felt like a Dominar again, but now, as they dragged him away and locked the security clamps across the cell-complex of his quarters, he realized he was wrong. Wrong to think they could ever understand. They would never treat him as a Dominar. Only a bigger fool. They weren't going to help him rescue Nyaella. They valued their own lives too highly. He would have to get her out on his own.

As the security clamps contracted, muscular sheets of skinsteel holding the door to his quarters in place, Rygel drew himself up to his full height. His face assumed an expression of sheer obstinacy.

He would not fail Nyaella again.

No matter what the cost.

Crichton had his pride and this hurt it—severely.

The last time he had gone cap in hand to anyone and asked for a decision to be reversed was in elementary school. Something to do with a bicycle seat and a car battery. Crichton hated times like this.

Then again, memory did that to you, he was beginning to learn. The human animal had a brain that was only so big, and although it was a wonderful organ with a near-infinite capacity for learning and knowing and imagining, sometimes it needed to shunt those old memories out of long-term storage and into the waste-bin.

He now stood in a world as far removed from his own as he could imagine. Nothing was the same here. He could take nothing for granted. Even the air he breathed came at a price. In this case, the air belonged to Jansz—one more way in which they were indebted to the Trader-Prime.

"You don't understand. We're willing to trade—whatever Jansz wants. Rygel . . . he . . . he's not really right in the head, you know? Kinda retarded. He likes to play emperor of the universe, but that's all just for show. Moya was a prison ship, you know . . . Rygel . . . he was on the psycho ward for . . . well, for years."

Vurid hugged the floor of the guest-anteroom a short distance away. His body quivered as Crichton spoke. He said nothing, merely listened.

"So you see, it's really not Rygel's fault . . . he's just, you know, kinda bent up here . . ." Crichton tapped the side of his head, a gesture that Vurid emulated curiously. ". . . He plays these games . . . we all have to make allowances. But, you know, we're really sorry he upset your boss, and, well, we certainly won't let him do it again."

Vurid said nothing.

"So, hey, whaddaya say? We got a trade or what?"

Crichton sneaked a look over his shoulder. Aeryn and Chiana said nothing. Zhaan smiled encouragingly. D'Argo, on the other hand, shook his head wearily. His view had been expressed unambiguously before they boarded the shuttle. *Kill everyone who does not help us.* It was a good theory, but unfortunately it essentially depended upon weapons they did not have. The Luxan's Qualta Blade was a class piece of technology—but there was no way on God's green Earth he could take on an entire fleet with it. And his Samurai attitude, though laudable in a battle scenario, would only get them all killed here and now. The odds were simply too great. Nope, Crichton assured himself, what was needed here was a shot of diplomacy—begging, actually.

Crichton shot a queasy smile at Vurid, then immediately froze. Eskimos meant "no" when they nodded, "yes" when they shook their heads. Would his smile be misinterpreted by the Facilitator? Maybe seen as some kind of insult?

Hey, man, lighten up. Don't go all paranoid on me. He bit down on his bad tooth. The pain was still a bitch, but it helped him focus.

Vurid gazed at Crichton. Six dark oval pupils locked on him like heatseekers. "Vurid hears your words. Lord Jansz disappointed by lack of respect shown by Moya party. May be hard to convince Lord Jansz to trade." The Facilitator's legs clicked against the deck plates as he shifted position, considering. "Vurid will present case for Moya party. Vurid not prepared to guarantee Lord Jansz's response. Moya party wait now."

The Facilitator scuttled from the room, stinger quivering. Crichton wondered at the significance of that. Did Vurid feel threatened? Was he afraid? Should they be afraid?

They were left to wait, for more than two hours. Hours in which Crichton began to wonder whether they were actually going to make it out of this one alive. Within ten minutes of their being left alone, D'Argo began to pace. This in itself was a bad sign. The big Luxan had suffered some bad knocks and was hardly famous for his patience. The fact that he was mumbling under his breath lit a red alert sign for Crichton.

With the tension level in the room notching itself to near breaking strain, Crichton finally exploded, "For crying out loud, D'Argo, will ya knock it off? You're driving me nuts."

D'Argo turned, his face knotted in anger. "I told Jansz the only thing I had to trade was your lives. You wouldn't want me to compromise my potential for trade would you? By damaging the goods."

"So it's clobberin' time, now, that it?" Crichton blew out his cheeks contemptuously—rather more so than he had intended, if he was honest. Still, it was too late to take it back now. "Well, my wise friend, I gotta tell ya . . ." and here Crichton surrendered fully to the anger building up inside, ". . . I ain't impressed. So you could punch me to jelly. Well hoorah for you. And what, precisely, would that achieve?"

D'Argo smiled humorlessly. "It would alleviate my anger—slightly."

Crichton felt his hands clench into fists. *Some days* . . .

"But we'd all be just as dead in the long run." Zhaan's voice was a breath of cool air amidst hot tempers. "You know that, both of you, so stop behaving like children."

Crichton unclenched his fists. *Zhaan was a vegetable, sure, but she set a good example.*

D'Argo, however, was not so easy to placate. "This is a matter between me and the human. You would be well advised to stay out of it."

"D'Argo, you're tense. We've all been on edge but there's no reason to . . ."

"Moya is dying! All of our lives are at risk. He is responsible. Tell me why I shouldn't just . . ."

"Because you're better than that. You don't need to kill, or even to hurt. If you do . . . well, I don't want to raise old ghosts but you'd be no better than those who murdered your wife."

D'Argo's eyes flashed murderously. He struggled for words. "How dare you . . ."

"I dare because I speak the truth!"

D'Argo's Qualta Blade was levelled at Zhaan. Crichton had seen the power of that weapon. Had seen it split stone, melt metal.

"D'Argo, man, you don't want to be doing that."

"Keep out of this, human. You're next."

"Oh yeah? What then? Kill Jansz? Blow up the universe? Eat Rygel for breakfast?"

D'Argo turned to face Crichton.

"Eat Rygel for breakfast?" he growled.

Crichton locked his jaw and tensed his body to move. Eyes locked on D'Argo's, he wondered whether he would be able to dodge the first blow, whether he would die cleanly, or whether he would merely lose a limb—

Hey! What the frak was going on?

Zhaan was trying to keep from smiling, but her eyes were dancing.

D'Argo had lowered his weapon. He was smiling!

"Eat Rygel for breakfast?" he roared with laughter.

Crichton swallowed hard with relief. "Yeah, I know. Pretty disgusting image, huh?"

"I do not understand you. You were faced with death. And yet you made a joke. I feel that I have witnessed something very wise—or clever—that I do not entirely understand." D'Argo shook his head.

Crichton didn't think he had been wise or clever—just lucky—but he held his tongue.

"Alright," D'Argo agreed. "We will wait. Just promise not to make any more distasteful culinary suggestions."

Crichton finally relaxed. Aeryn, he noticed, had also lowered her rifle, but Chiana had backed into a corner of the chamber and was regarding them all warily—eyes narrowed, body taut. Fight or flight. *Hell*, thought Crichton, *we must have scared her grotless*.

Crichton held out his hand to her. "Chiana, look, I'm sorry if we upset you. We were just, you know, blowing off steam."

"You all need to just blez out."

"Yeah, well, good idea."

Pilot's voice came over Zhaan's comm. "I don't mean to alarm you, but Moya is worsening. You must expedite the necessary trade agreement with Jansz at greatest speed."

"Pilot, this is Aeryn. How long do we have?"

"A matter of arns, I'm afraid. The necrosis has spread throughout large areas of Moya's central nervous system. Soon, she will be unable to sustain life."

"Alright. We're working on it."

"I know you are."

At this moment the door to the guest antechamber opened and Vurid scuttled through. He seemed even more agitated than when he had left. Without any preamble, he headed straight for Crichton.

"Vurid has spoken with Lord Jansz. Lord Jansz graciously agrees to trade. Bearing in mind prior . . . matters of etiquette . . . price has increased."

"OK, yeah, so what are we talking here? A few more albums? I got a whole bunch."

"Price for Moya cure is now . . ." Vurid turned and pointed with two of his four hands directly at Chiana, ". . . this individual."

There was a momentary silence. Then, the air was filled with shocked, outraged voices:

". . . outta your freakin' mind, pal, if you think we're gonna . . ."

". . . mercenary enough to trade one of our own for . . ."

". . . be highly immoral and as such is . . ."

". . . what are you now, slavers, or . . ."

"Shut up! Why don't you all just shut the frell up for once!" All heads turned. The furious voice was Chiana's. Hands on hips, face contorted in anger, her porcelain skin was flushed a darker color.

Crichton frowned. *Why was she so upset? It wasn't as if they had been about to trade her off for some . . .*

But Chiana was just getting wound up. "Who the frell do you think you are to make decisions for me?" she raged. "Why would I want to stay on a doomed ship with a bunch of greebols who argue all day and night? You know what? You're all tinked!" Chiana paused for breath.

"I thought it would be a really dag-yo adventure to travel with you. Boy, was I ever frelling wrong! I'll take my chances with Jansz." Without another word, Chiana ran across the chamber, and stood next to Vurid.

Vurid appeared pleased. Managing to look in six different directions at once, he said, "Vurid is grateful that negotiations are concluded with success. Arrangements will be made to supply Moya embryo to Lord Jansz's laboratory. Moya party will be informed when T-cell treatment is available for use. Lord Jansz thanks Moya party and looks forward to future trade. That is all."

Moments later Vurid and Chiana were gone.

To Crichton, the whole scene had taken place with a kind of dreamlike surrealism. Funny, he thought, how in just a moment everything could change. That's all it had taken—a moment, and now it was goodbye Chiana. Though they were aware that she lied, cheated, and stole, she was also young and emotionally fragile. The rest of the crew, except perhaps for Rygel, all felt rather protective toward her. A little renki, Pilot called her—a cheeky little imp. How she could willingly cast her lot with Jansz was incomprehensible. But, Chiana was a survivor . . .

Well, what was done was done. It was out of their control now.

"The Magnificent Seven," Crichton mused quietly.

D'Argo glanced questioningly at Crichton.

"That's how many we are now. You, me, Aeryn, Zhaan, Rygel, Moya and Pilot. *The Magnificent Seven*—it's a movie."

Rygel hovered in the tertiary access artery, a short distance from his quarters. Moya was silent and still—dying—but Rygel was focused on, what were for him, more important matters.

For a moment, he thought about his incarcerators. Would they never learn? The simple matter of the biological composition of Moya's skinsteel walls coupled with his own involuntary enzyme secretions meant he would never be held captive in his former prison again, so long as he could sweat.

Passing through a locked door had been the least of his worries. Escaping from prison cells was not so different.

No. Escape from his quarters was not an issue. What concerned him now was how to reach Nyaella.

If he tried to use Moya's shuttle he would be seen and in all likelihood stopped. Space suits were expensive commodities this far from the Commerce Lanes—in any case, even if he could find one designed to fit his splendid pear-shaped physique, he would probably not be able to afford it. No one onboard had any money right now. And although his drafts might once have been drawn on the richest banks of the Hynerian empire, they were no more than scrap paper in the Uncharted Territories. And in

these parts, credit was synonymous with the most offensive of swear words.

So, how to get from Moya to Jansz's flagship, without a shuttle and without a space suit? If he did not
manage to rescue Nyaella before a cure was found for
Moya then all would be lost. Well, he was a Dominar,
was he not? He'd overcome greater obstacles, endured
more desperate situations. Yes, Rygel was sure he'd
come up with something.

Wait a minute.

A cure for Moya.

What was it they'd needed? An embryo?

Rygel's eyes gleamed and he smiled slyly. The smile
that came whenever he was about to get his own way.

Jansz sent his tugs to fit Moya with grappling lines and
draw her close to his vessel. Dressed in hooks and ca-
bles, the Leviathan lay meekly alongside the Trader-
Prime's flagship. Her hull pulsed softly, painfully. Her
weakened pulse signalled that her life was slowly
ebbing away . . .

A small legion of medics trod through Moya's
chambers.

Instruments flashed in the darkness, minds gathered
information and spun eagerly upon a line of thought:
the necrosis was spreading fast. They needed T-cells—
an egg must be retrieved immediately.

Inside the dying starship, standing guard over the
medics, D'Argo paced. He was unnerved by the
strange silence. He had grown used to the myriad
sounds that made it clear they were aboard a living
ship. Moya was his refuge and, in a way, he, too, felt a

symbiosis with her—though, of course, not a real symbiosis such as Moya and Pilot shared.

D'Argo paced. Though no longer a Peacekeeper prisoner, he still wasn't in control of his life. Now, time was his ruthless master. Time that continued to melt away while Moya came closer and closer to death. Time that disappeared with no trace of his son. Time lost forever. D'Argo cursed its passing with every breath.

For D'Argo, only his engagement in battle seemed to lessen his feelings of regret, of mistakes, of endless guilt. But there was no battle. No rush of blood to blank the mind. Not now. It was too quiet.

Too quiet!

D'Argo's feet hammered the skinsteel artery; boot heels penetrating deeply, tracks that would normally have filled and smoothed with the pulse of blood through veins, but that now remained visible reminders of his anger and Moya's precarious condition.

While he paced, the medics continued to probe for a healthy unquickened egg; the glutinous nodule of undifferentiated T-cells with which to produce a cure for Moya.

Moya had already borne a single child, Talyn, progeny of war and peace, conceived in love and quickened by Peacekeeper technology. A living gunship with a child's mind, controlled now by Captain Crais, a renegade Peacekeeper who was obsessed with capturing Moya and her crew.

Where was Crais now? Surely, they were easy prey now. Perhaps he was waiting for Moya to be cured before delivering the final blow. At times, D'Argo thought he would welcome that blow when it came, for it would bring peace, final, eternal. Until then . . .

D'Argo's mind needed to forget the past and yet everything he saw reminded him of it.

A medic's laser
(killer's knife)
scalpel flashed in the silence of
(his home)
Moya's
(heart)
womb.

Split, Moya surrendered the life within to medics who wrapped the steaming egg in snug metal, bearing it far from D'Argo's sight. Suddenly, he was there, right there, living the hideous memories, seeing the open door, the blood-spattered floor, and her body on the floor—why was she lying on the floor like that? Had she fallen? But no, there was no denying the sight, the smell of blood, of death. And D'Argo had screamed then, the pitiful sound of an animal torn from life and cast into infinite terror and blackness.

D'Argo fell heavily against the artery wall; head pounding with old memories. But the scream—that was real enough; he knew it when Aeryn and the medics turned to look at him, she with shocked concern, the rest merely with curiosity.

Instantly, Aeryn was by his side. "Don't worry. I'll be alright," he assured her.

The look from the medics seemed to say: Is this Luxan mad?

To be alone.

A selfish need, but one essential to wellbeing. And

not without precedent. The dekacycle spent in the ice-monasteries of Ygaan had taught well. A priest of sound mind and spirit could attend the needs of others. A priest racked by tensions, distracted from purity of focus by fear, anger, and guilt, most definitely could not.

Zhaan stood quietly in Moya's observation blister, feet rooted in the photosynthetic organic mulch that carpeted the chamber and provided, under normal circumstances, a source of nourishment for the star-going Leviathan. Moya currently faced away from the trader fleet; from this angle the sky appeared strangely empty though filled with light from a nearby star—the blue supergiant—spectacularly featured in the nearspace field. Cold fire filled the blister and splashed across its lone occupant. Arms held wide, head back and eyes tilted upwards, Zhaan regarded the supergiant with mixed emotions. The star was nearing the end of its life, a dangerously unstable condition that spelled certain death for any planetary inhabitants . . . yet while it still shone, its photonic presence produced a mixture of strong emotions within her—chief among them, joy.

Zhaan had a particular affinity for light. Light was life, and that meant life in the direct, sexual way. For light stimulated birth and growth and movement and learning. The light of her own star had propelled Zhaan's species from a humble vegetative origin to sentience and space flight. From an organism that responded only to mindless chemical stimuli, to one that could define and seek the presence of God. Oh, yes. Light had raised Zhaan to the stars, and for that she was grateful.

Now one such star—the ancient supergiant—bathed

her in its cold fire, indigo radiance accentuating her exotic azure skin and ice-blue eyes, blue within blue within blue . . . and as her skin soaked up the sparse photonic energy, so her mind responded with the appropriate emotional pattern. The warmest feelings came from the hottest stars. Yellow main sequence stars were able to stimulate the pleasure centre of her brain, yielding continuous, uncontrollable orgasm. Pulsing quasars like spinning tops brought a childlike delight, making her giggle uncontrollably. Brown dwarfs—the stillborn ghosts of suns that never were—stirred within her a feeling of overwhelming sadness, while the duller, larger, redder suns brought more constant emotions . . . love and anger prominent among them, slow fire both.

This time the feeling was different. The blue supergiant was colder, more distant, a huge presence looming on her personal horizon, distorting her emotional equilibrium as it might have dominated the field of view for any being that observed the universe through just its eyes. The feeling engendered by this ancient source of photonic energy was not exactly fear, nor was it quite joy . . . more like apprehension. Or possibly expectation. Or maybe the expectation was a secondary emotion, one that itself yielded the joy of feelings never before experienced.

Though she had lived many dekacycles, Zhaan had never before experienced a sun like this. Never before encountered such a precise and yet overpowering emotional range. She had no words for the feelings that coursed through her pores, soaked into her core, drifted as dream-particles through the photosynthetic chemical processors that were her lungs. Nothing in her experience had ever touched her like this. Oh, she had experienced joy, fear, anger, the nova-release of bold young stars . . . but never this combination of age and complexity . . . never this sheer sophistication.

Zhaan prepared to embrace the emotional release. Skin trembled, stomata gulped air and light; quiveringly close to sporulation, and then . . .

Zhaan gasped. Not ecstasy: pain.

Moya shuddered. Skinsteel and alumuscle slid across escarpment bones, grinding.

Zhaan had come here to find a brief respite from the tension of the last days; to pray for Moya, to dare to hope for life in the cruellest depths of space.

Her prayers remained unanswered, her hope unfulfilled.

Pilot's voice came over her comm. It was so weak as to be almost a whisper. Symbiotically linked to the great Leviathan, he was dying too.

"Moya requests your presence here in the control nexus. She knows she is dying and asks that you administer the Imtoch s'Reen."

Zhaan shuddered, trying to pull her senses back from the photon-drenched perfection of starspace, trying to focus on what Pilot was saying.

Imtoch s'Reen—the last rites. Zhaan sank to her knees, then collapsed on the mulchy floor. Fear and anger chased each other around the inside of her head, the emotions growing as the hold of the blue supergiant subsided. Unquickened pollen clouded the air in drifts, shocked from her still-trembling skin. It sank in sparkling curls to the ground, to be absorbed by the mulch and eventually converted into biomass on which Moya might one day feed.

If she lived.

When Zhaan spoke, her voice trembled with anger. "I'll come to the nexus, Pilot. But I will not administer last rites. Moya is not going to die. And that's my last word."

There were three embryos stasis-locked by Peacekeeper technology in Moya's birth chamber. The embryos were shuttle-sized cell-nodules, locked after fertilization but before mitosis had taken place. Technology seeds had been implanted that, when quickened, would grow into weapons pods of the kind Moya's first offspring, Talyn, had been born with.

Rygel shuddered at the thought of Talyn's name. His birth had been a shock to everyone.

Deciding which embryo to hide inside had not been easy. Checking the condition-readouts yielded a library of digital codes and a smattering of useful information. Playing the odds, Rygel eventually selected the embryo nearest the fallopian tunnel. For an object of its size there was only one way out of the chamber—and that was the way nature had intended it to go.

The embryo was larger than a short-range shuttle even before cell-differentiation. It was a huge mass composed of multiple-sourced organic DNA and self-replicating high-tech packets. Hiding one more inert box—a box just a whisker larger than a burly Hynerian, say—among such a complex artifact had proven to be no problem at all.

The only worry had come when Rygel realized the journey time might outlast the available air supply. He had shrugged as best he could within the limited space of the concealing box. A Dominar's life was inevitably one of risk and glory. No risk—no glory.

The journey had been strangely disorienting—within the box he was in pitch darkness—and also disturbing, for he could not help but be reminded of the dreadful time following the uprising, when he had been held prisoner for so long in the darkness of—

Avoiding the thought, Rygel expended every last effort in trying to remain calm.

The embryo was loaded onto the medical skiff and made its short journey across space.

Now a concealed hatch in the box opened and a pair of wary eyes peered out, followed by a relieved sigh. The eyes backed up information provided by a limited passive-sensor scan performed by instrumentation concealed in his ThroneSled.

The room—large, circular, white tiled—was lined with data acquisitors, none of which were yet active. White-suited medics moved purposefully through a maze of technology. Analysis and replication equipment, distilleries, chemical farms . . . in a manner common to theorists of any species, so intent were the medics upon the readings from their instruments that no one paid the slightest attention to the actual object under examination.

Rygel couldn't repress a sly smile. So far, the odds were playing out in his favor.

The small Hynerian crept from the box, his ThroneSled powered down in order to conceal its presence from potential scans. Almost immediately he found himself face to face with a large tank containing a curious creature—perhaps many creatures, it was hard to say. Something like a pink snail peered at him from beneath an urchin-like layer of worms. The creature was held within the tank by a web of glass probes. Fluids bubbled gently within the tubes. Chemical solutions. Were they being injected or extracted? Rygel shuddered, thinking of Nyaella. The creature's eyes locked on his. Could it see him? Was it aware of his presence? Its limbs stirred, agitated movement. Was it trying to give the alarm? Did it want his help?

Rygel hovered indecisively. This creature was beyond his help—perhaps it was just as well as it was clearly unintelligent. He could only hope that whatever they were doing with it involved a considerable degree of anesthetic.

Turning, he lifted the ThroneSled with an effort—it was engineered from light but highly tensile material—and waddled quickly from the room.

No one saw him go.

Some days it paid to be small.

In a small fruit and vegetable stall in the main marketplace, some way from the industrial sections of the ship, Rygel paused to take stock. So far so good. But there was still a lot of ground to cover. To reach Nyaella. To figure out a way to get her off Jansz's ship and onto Moya. And all without being noticed. His lips moved as he mentally explored options. Grand Vizier Noonspurner had been known to advise that talking to oneself could be a sign of madness. But, as Rygel had come to realize, he was frequently the only one qualified to understand himself or—if he was truthful—the only one prepared to listen.

"Yo, man, check it out, it's a talking pear."

"Don' look none too edible to me, bro'."

"Nah, man, don' you be fool. These star fruit are rumbustuous when they sliced and fried. You go on an' pick it up now, you hear?"

"You the boss."

Rygel turned slowly, bringing the weighty gaze of the ruler of empires to bear on the market-goers who had disturbed him. Two balls of yellow fur were regarding him from two vast cyclops eyes.

"Bro', check it out—the pear got eyes. It *wink* at me!"

Rygel examined his hecklers quickly for any sign of a weapon. Or limbs. None being in evidence, he regained a measure of confidence. He allowed his ThroneSled to raise itself to eye height. "I'll do more than wink at you if you utter one more word about slicing and frying," he said imperiously.

The yellow balls of fur quivered. Eyelids like saucepan lids blinked nervously.

"Oh, yes. I've got . . . *spines,*" Rygel blustered. "They're poisonous. I'll stick them in your throat and puncture your stomach and give you septic ulcers for a month!"

The yellow-furred creatures shivered.

"Yeah, well, we sorry for the presumption an' all but you look like fruit to us."

"Sure do. But hey, we gon' leave you 'lone now. Eat well, you hear?"

"We gone now."

"Outtahere."

"Flipside."

"Don' you be followin' us now."

"Live and let fry, that's our motto."

The two yellow-furred creatures vanished into the crowd.

Rygel sighed as the tension drained from his body. Life was full of close encounters like this. Tiny moments sent to try your patience and keep you from your goals. Beginning to feel more relaxed, Rygel

emerged from the stall and began to make his way
through the marketplace—only to feel his ThroneSled
tip backwards as a huge hand closed into a fist across
its stern rail.

"You gonna buy those or what?"

Rygel spun in his chair. The proprietor of the fruit
store loomed behind him.

"Buy?" Rygel spluttered indignantly. "Buy what?
Has everyone in this fleet gone completely mad?"

The stall owner hooked one gargantuan finger into
Rygel's ThroneSled. It emerged with twenty or so
small fruits. Rygel stared. "Those . . . It was those yellow prabatkos . . . those . . . I'll boil them in oil!"

The stall owner stared.

Rygel said, "You must have seen them. Yellow furry
things with one big eye each. Terrible accents. Common as muck."

The stall owner considered. "The Yzzies? They
planted this lot on you?"

"Why yes, of course. Now if you would . . ."

"Well, that was pretty clever of them, don't you
think?" The stall owner lowered his voice to a threatening rumble. "Considering they don't have any
hands."

Rygel licked his lips. Why couldn't things ever just
be simple? "Well, now you mention it, no, you're
right, they didn't just . . . Look. I'm sorry. I'll pay for
the fruit. I just have to go . . . uh . . . back to my spaceship and . . . well, look. I'll be back before you know
it. I've got a huge account you know. Mountains of
gold. Honestly. Pleasure doing business with you! Bye
now!"

And urging the ThroneSled to a sudden burst of

maximum power, Rygel managed to break free from the stall owner's grip and lose himself in the crowd. The stall owner's angry shouts quickly became part of the background melee. Only when the voice was indistinguishable from the general hubbub of the marketplace, did Rygel breathe a sigh of relief.

So he looked like a pear did he? Emperor of six hundred billion souls—a *pear? Let it go. There are more important considerations.*

His father's words, from so long ago—words once hated—but now Rygel knew them for their true worth. *A Dominar must never be eclipsed by his own shadow.* But what if he was no longer Dominar? What bound him then—what rules or code or morality? Was he anything more than the criminal he had been taken for for so long?

Rygel's features set in absolute determination. His skin smoothed right out around his eyes and took on a slippery sheen of sheer obstinacy. There was only one thing he needed right now. One action to take. One soul to save.

One dream to bring from the shadows into the light.

Her name was Nyaella.

CHAPTER 5

She was still just where he had left her. *What kind of devil could keep a Hynerienne chained up like this, with no warm pools of water to soak in, no perfume to anoint her still magnificent body?*

"Nyaella."

"Rygel. I knew you would come."

"How could I not."

She rose from the bed, a vision in pearlescent green, her skin and eyes glowing—if anything, even more deliciously creased than he remembered.

"Kiss me."

"I don't deserve to."

"You are a Dominar. You deserve anything you want."

"Perhaps it's the chains, then." Rygel sighed. "Do you have any other clothes here?"

A smile hung trembling from her lips. "I seem to remember a younger Rygel who was more interested in *removing* my clothes . . ."

Rygel snorted in embarrassment. He pulled a robe from some tissue paper.

"Stolen?"

"Traded. You can get anything on this ship."

"Yes, it's an amazing place."

"Nyaella, you must tell me everything that's happened to you, but not until we get out of here. Then we'll have time for wine—and endless kisses."

"How do I get free?" The chains clinked delicately as Nyaella shrugged.

Rygel pulled out a pair of cutters. *That Crichton had some amazing tools*. "Not exactly high-tech, but I think they'll do the trick."

"Oh, Rygel, you're as clever as ever."

Rygel cut the chains and Nyaella was free. He wanted to take her in his arms, but that would have to wait.

"Hurry, Nyaella. Put on this robe."

"There's something I have to do first." Nyaella's eyes were wide. Her scent was strong.

As was the blow she aimed at his head. Rygel staggered.

"Are you completely fahrbot?" Rygel shouted. He didn't know if he was more shocked or hurt. "What's that for?"

"That's for leaving me without a word!" A quick kick from Nyaella had Rygel howling in pain. A torrent of blows followed in fast succession. "And so is this, and this, and this!"

"Nyaella, wait, I—I'm sure there would be those who would pay handsomely to be kicked by a scantily clad Hynerienne, but—ooh!—what was that for?"

Her voice was a throaty growl. "Same thing!"

"Oh." Rygel sat up groaning. "Clearly I have a lot to apologize for."

Nyaella tossed on the robe he had brought. "Consider us even."

"That will be my . . ." Rygel rubbed his arm and winced, "pleasure." The bruised Hynerian clambered into his ThroneSled, groaning. His body wasn't reluctant to let him know how badly it was hurt—and in just how many places.

"I would not want you as an enemy, Nyaella."

"Just get me out of here, Rygel. You won't believe how grateful I can be."

"Alright. Get on."

"Do you have any idea how long I've waited for that invitation?" Her words came with a smile—but one that Rygel could not decipher. Rygel glanced both ways along the corridor. Why was it deserted? Where were the vendors? Was it some sort of holiday?

Something was making him uneasy. Had he forgotten something?

"Yo, lookit what we got here."

Oh, what the yotz now?

"Right—the talking pear."

"Yo, man, you a hard pear to find."

A ball of bright yellow fur blocked his path. He swung the sled around. A second ball of fur blocked any retreat.

"Joy to see you."

"Yeah. Real joy."

Rygel got the feeling it was not pleasure that filled the Yzzies' voices. He sighed. *Some days it was just one thing after another.* "You common frodank deviants never learn, do you?"

Nyaella tugged at his arm. "Don't mess with these guys, Rygel. They're heavy."

"On the contrary. They're yellow and furry and don't have any arms. What threat can they possibly pose?"

"S'alri. Give us our fruit and we be gone."

"Yeah. Fruit."

Rygel felt his anger building. "I don't have any fruit."

"You lookin' after fruit for us."

"Our fruit."

"In there."

Rygel felt his anger rising. "Of course. Why else would I have surrendered an empire and suffered hundreds of cycles of incarceration and torture if not to help you steal rotting fruit from a greebol of an arcade vendor?" The anger in Rygel's voice rose with each word.

Nyaella's arms tightened nervously around his waist.

"You not have fruit?"

"We need fruit."

"Need it bad."

"Get me?"

Rygel blinked. For yellow furballs the Yzzies could be intense. "Most of it the vendor took back. The rest I traded for clothes."

The Yzzies exchanged cyclopean glances. "Hear that?"

"Oh, yeah."

"Talking pear trade our fruit."

"For clothes."

"Too bad, I guess."

"Too bad, yeah—for talking pear."

The next few moments were confused. Rygel heard a peculiar sound—that of escaping air or perhaps incredibly deep breathing—and suddenly the Yzzies were twice, now three times their normal size. Their fur was standing out on end, only it wasn't fur, he now realized—more like spines. Sharp spines. Something like black oil glinted at the tips.

Nyaella punched him. "I told you not to antagonize them!"

"You don' have fruit. Tha's OK."

"You give us cash instead. We buy fruit."

"Yeah. Cash."

"Cash for fruit."

"All you got."

"Right now."

The Yzzies sidled closer. Threatening.

"The spines are poisonous." Nyaella's voice was a whisper. "Fast-acting neurotoxin. No antidote."

"Unless talking pear want to rumble?"

Rygel frowned. "Now look here. There's no need for any trouble. You want money? Fine. I have money."

"Not plastic, man."

"Give us cash."

"Cash for fruit."

"Cash or your life."

The Yzzies crowded close, spines hissing sibilantly as they rubbed together. One particularly long spine oozed black oil a finger's width from Rygel's flat nose.

"I get the point."

"Make sure you do."

"Mess with us and we spike you, man."

"Spike you good."

"Now give us cash."

"Cash!"

"Now!"

Rygel took something from his ThroneSled. A money pouch. "I've been saving this for a sunny day," he said. "It's all I have. Are you sure you want it?"

"Open bag!"

"Open now!"

"Give!"

Rygel opened. Rygel gave.

The Yzzies screamed.

"Hang on!"

Nyaella's arms tightened reflexively around Rygel's round belly as he gunned the ThroneSled's anti-gravs. Vehicle and occupants flew upwards, careened off the ceiling and tore off down the corridor, leaving two balls of yellow fluff, blind eyes streaming, howling agonized curses in their wake.

"What *was* that?"

"My sweat pad."

"Your sweat pad?"

"I keep it in a money pouch because it's precious beyond all wealth."

"Why?"

Rygel continued in a none-too-modest lecture hall tone. "I discovered many cycles ago that enzymes in Hynerian sweat can make holes in Leviathan prison cells." He shrugged; the ThroneSled tipped, then righted itself. "The discovery that these enzymes also seem to act like powerful tear gas on certain aggressive life forms is a more recent discovery."

Rygel slowed the ThroneSled to a moderate walking pace so as to preserve anonymity and eased his way out into the marketplace crowd.

He was very pleased with himself.

Now all they had to do was—

"There he is! There's the blotching thief who stole my fruit!"

"I see you haven't lost your gift for making friends." Nyaella swore as the stall owner ran towards them, outsize limbs thumping ponderously as he came.

"Move it, Rygel!" Nyaella screamed.

Minutes later, Rygel and Nyaella had left the wildly gesticulating stall owner behind. They were moving along the ceiling of the marketplace, weaving between hanging baskets of ferns, lit from above by the brilliance of the spiral nebula, now replaced by the huge, cold presence of the nearby blue supergiant star.

Rygel found his eyes locked to the star.

Something about that star . . . something was . . . he shook his head, aware that Nyaella was speaking.

"Are you listening to me? I said, what are we going to do now? What's your plan for getting out of here?"

"Plan?"

"Beyond skulking around like a rodent, I mean."

"Well . . ." Rygel licked his lips.

"Fine. I take it that means you have no plan."

"Uh. I had planned to go back to Moya the same way I came. On the medical shuttle."

"And what were you planning to hide inside this

time? Someone's wallet? A small protein tube full of cloned enzymes?"

"Well, I thought we could, you know . . ."

"What? Get captured and tortured again? I see. Well, I must congratulate you, Rygel. The years have not dimmed your brilliant wit nor, indeed, your stunning foresight."

"Now there's no need for sarcasm . . ."

"But every need for a swift escape! So listen to me. Here's what we'll do . . ."

As Rygel listened to her words, his ears stuck right out and quivered—not merely because of apprehension, but outright fear, too.

Ten minutes later they were standing in the middle of one of the largest stalls in the market. A place where, it seemed, one could buy or barter anything from oxygen to glue, from space suits to sextants, propellant to gyroscopes to comms to radstrips to hard tack. In short, anything one might conceivably need if one were part of a space-going community that rarely, if ever, saw the surface of a planet and spent much of the time by choice in a hard vacuum.

"You want to swap *what?*"

The proprietor of the stall was humanoid to nine parts, disturbingly like Crichton in that it was big and dry and—even among this insane crowd of hawkers and barkers and punters—far too loud. Unlike Crichton this creature was a female. At least Rygel thought it was a female. With humanoids it was so difficult to tell.

"For *what?*" the proprietor shrieked.

"This. It's a ThroneSled. It belonged to a Dominar of the Hynerian Empire."

"Oh." The female seemed to muster a little interest. "Royal artifact, huh? Find it prospecting, did you? Congratulations. It's very pretty. Does it do anything? I run a practical shop: no frivolities or luxuries here. A thing's no good if doesn't do something, you know."

Rygel blinked. *How could this dumb nurfer not recognize that this was the choice trade opportunity of a lifetime?*

"Short of an actual Dominar," Rygel pronounced haughtily, "this is the most precious thing the Hynerian Empire ever produced."

"That so? One of a kind? Limited edition? Had a rocket here once. Marvelous piece of equipment. Moved like greased lightning, let me tell you—oh yeah—right off my floor and into a franging crater. Frelling Peacekeepers. So all fired up to stop every bit of creative trade except their own. Makes you want to take a wrench to the lot of 'em. Sorry—rambling, I know. You were saying? This some kind of limited-production run?"

"A definite one of its kind. It's passed down through sixteen generations of Hynerian rulers."

The proprietor grinned. "Guess the seat's a bit worn then, huh?"

"The anti-gravs alone are worth a king's ransom, let alone what you might acquire from an interested collector of antiquities. The ThroneSled's actual worth is incalculable."

"Maybe you'd be better off taking it to a museum, then. I hear there's one on Snapdragon—little Class K star about three or four arns from here."

Rygel groaned. At this rate he'd be old enough to qualify for a pension before he could conclude a deal, let alone escape from Jansz's frelling flagship. Moya would have been cured and sailed away and had a hundred offspring before this female ran out of breath.

"Well, the thing is, you see, I happen to be in a spot of financial bother. I'm quite willing to let the ThroneSled go for, oh, say two-thirds of its market value—to a discerning engineer such as yourself. You may be able to use its parts. The graviton inductor is only fifty cycles old—practically brand new."

"Well, I can verify that with a metallo-crystallography scan. Molecules don't lie, you know."

"I'm very relieved to hear it."

"So are most ship engineers, let me tell you. Now then, as to your proposed trade . . ."

The proprietor rubbed grease-stained fingers across the bridge of her nose, leaving black marks that resembled war paint. "Alright. You're asking way too much for it . . . but let's assume we might—only *might*, let me emphasize—have a trade here. What would you be wanting in exchange?"

"I presume you keep environment suits as part of your manifest?"

"Only the best."

"For Hynerians?"

"As you can see."

"How much?"

The humanoid named a figure.

Rygel gulped. On Hyneria such a sum would have bought him a small province—and the servants to run it.

"What about second-hand ones?"

The proprietor shook her head. "No such thing as a second-hand space suit out here. Not unless you got breakdown and after sales support from your species' god."

"You have a point." Rygel considered.

Nyaella elbowed him in the ribs. "Come on. Get on with it! I remember you being more decisive than this!"

"Alright, then. What about that?"

"My old Lifebuoy? You want my old Lifebuoy?"

"Does it work?"

"Of course it does. Air's extra, though."

"Why am I not surprised?"

"You want to swap your shiny new ThroneSled for my old Lifebuoy. Well. I never did! Hey roGuerr!" The female shouted to the second humanoid working the stall. "Guess what?"

Rygel had visions of every trader in the marketplace and his brother and sister queuing up for a look at the latest mark.

"Do we have a trade or should I ask for directions to the museum on Snapdragon?" Rygel demanded.

The humanoid considered. "That Lifebuoy saved my life, you know."

"There's no point in pushing. I don't have anything else to trade."

"It's alright. I like you. I ain't gonna rip you off. Not too much, anyway. Now—show me what this shiny new ThroneSled of mine can do."

Minutes later, a weary-looking Rygel shook hands to seal the deal. Nyaella took one side of the Lifebuoy, he took the other and they waddled off along the corridor at the best speed they could muster.

"This idea of yours better work," Rygel muttered.

"I expected something a little more expedient from the richest individual in the Second Quadrant."

Rygel frowned. "Regretfully, at this juncture, I am a Dominar in name only."

Nyaella snuffled impatiently. "Just so long as you programmed your 'puter accurately. Now come on. We've got ten minutes to reach the garbage chute rendezvous."

Five minutes after Rygel and Nyaella had waddled off, the humanoid female known as deNeese lifted the ThroneSled onto the counter and uttered a satisfied chuckle. "Finally ditched that old Peacekeeper Lifebuoy. Thought we were gonna be stuck with that sucker for a lifetime."

Her partner, the robust and hairy roGuerr, stepped alongside deNeese, pulling the stall awning closed and latching it as he did so. "Think the little guy knew what a hot potato he was selling?"

"I know one thing. Any decent political officer would pay through the nose for the specs on this baby. Hynerian technology is one of the most closely guarded secrets in the seven sectors."

"Goddamn, baby, it's our meal ticket outta this tub," roGuerr replied, laughing. "Fire it up again, will ya? Let's see what other juicy tidbits 'Slippery When Wet' left in the ROM."

"Sure."

With a chuckle, deNeese thumbed the boot-up stud.

Acting on Rygel's pre-programmed instructions, the ThroneSled whirled, flew straight at the awning, tore a flapping gap in the cloth and vanished into the thronging market crowd.

"Holy dren!"

"Little green bastard ripped us off!"

Surprise was quickly replaced by anger.

"Gonna stand for that?"

"Hell, no!"

"I'll get the guns."

Some distance from the furious stall owners, Rygel and Nyaella stood beside the returned ThroneSled, attempting to puzzle out the mechanism of the Peacekeeper Lifebuoy. The garbage disposal area was little more than a large metal room full of noxious and festering refuse that was periodically emptied into space. To conserve power, the space-doors were opened infrequently. Rygel thought he saw something move among the rubbish. Something slimy and not too small. Several somethings.

"I can't see a power reading, Nyaella."

"It's automatic. There must be one."

"You mean it only comes on in a vacuum?"

"I suppose."

"How would anyone ever check it was working?"

"Good point."

"This is a piece of junk. That frelling crook ripped us off."

A Hynerian of his not-exactly-tender years shouldn't have to surrender his ThroneSled and walk—not even to pull off the escape of the dekacycle. Rygel had the sickening feeling he had been outfoxed. As he straightened up, his eyes met those of the humanoid in question and her partner . . . and the nozzles of their guns.

"Oh, frak," the Dominar of six hundred billion souls muttered softly.

"This is no time for swearing, Rygel. Help me to get this—oh!" Nyaella, too, saw the cold eyes and the colder gun muzzles. "Frak."

"You activate it with the little yellow button," roGuerr told them. "There, on the side."

Rygel nodded, feeling sick.

"Shame you're never going to get a chance to use it," deNeese added, in the same chilly tone.

Rygel smiled weakly. "I don't suppose your deals come with a money-back guarantee?"

Their thumbs tightened on the firing studs. Words did not seem necessary.

A sudden noise made deNeese whirl. "Rog, look out!"

Twin screeches of alarm preceded the appearance of two dangerously inflated balls of black-tipped yellow spines.

"It's the bloody Yzzies!"

"Yo, can the guns!"

"Can guns or we spike you, too!"

"Talking pear our mark."

"Owes us big-time."

"Hell, 'Neese, it's a trap! The damn frog lured us here!"

"You know what's on those spines?"

"It ain't your gran's old shampoo. Watch it!"

Rygel and Nyaella's eyes were riveted on the guns and spines waving menacingly back and forth.

"Can guns now!"

"Hell with that, buddy!"

"Do it or we spike you!"

"Clarn off or we shoot you!"

"Yzz not play game here!"

"Yeah? We not play game either, grolash!"

"Talking pear owes us!"

"Damn frog owes *us!*"

Rygel had faced many difficult situations in his life. But none had quite prepared him for seeing two sets of guns and about a thousand poison-tipped spines all turned in his direction.

Nyaella had edged herself behind Rygel.

He licked his lips nervously. "Now . . . there's no need to overreact . . . I'm sure we can . . . I mean, we're all mature individuals so I have no doubt we can . . ." He blinked. "Oh frak," he finished. How unseemly it would be if this was the last word on his lips.

Though generations of Hynerian rulers before him had set religious temples upon their highest hills and widest ponds, Rygel had always walked his own path through life's maze of conflicting beliefs. Until this point in his life, he had neither believed in nor endorsed the existence of any kind of deity. But maybe he had been wrong. For in that moment of almost certain death, fate had intervened—in the form of one furious, fruit stall vendor. Determined to be compensated for his stolen goods, he burst into the refuse dump, screaming angrily and waving his neurostunner at Rygel. This was a fatal mistake. Both humanoids and Yzzies turned.

Flames burst from their guns.

The vendor fell, blood spurting from his chest and severed arm.

In practically the same moment, ricocheting bullets caught first one and then both angry yellow balls. They burst into spectacular flames, spraying the entire room with chunks of bloody meat and a hail of deadly spines.

Five agonized screams.

Five corpses lay among the rubbish.

Rygel and Nyaella could barely see through the smoke.

Flames licked eagerly at the refuse.

Rygel and Nyaella emerged from behind a metal storage drum, noting the carnage in shocked silence. Rygel carefully removed a piece of rotting fruit peel from his ear.

Several piles of rubbish were burning out of control. They would have to dash through the smoke and flames and around a burning mountain of garbage to reach the doors.

"Nyaella, I really think we should leave. *Now!*"

Six hours passed uneventfully—for all except Moya, whose necrosis, though somewhat slower now, was still progressing at a frightening pace.

The crew could do nothing but wait until Jansz's apothecaries produced a cure. The stress they all felt as they waited and watched the arns tick away, microt by microt, exacerbated everyone's anxiety. Tempers were short and nerves on edge.

D'Argo and Aeryn came close to squaring off with clenched fists after a discussion concerning embryo termination somehow transformed into a stand-up shouting match on the subject of interracial marriages, murder, kidnap, and Peacekeeper morality.

Crichton was tired of playing negotiator. They could kill each other for all he cared at the moment. He decided to take a look around Chiana's quarters. Surprisingly, she had left empty-handed. Well, this was a chance to see what she'd been salting away in there. He wouldn't be surprised if his missing CDs showed up.

Aeryn stopped at Chiana's doorway and looked in. "Just because she's gone, you think you can riffle through her belongings?"

"You wouldn't say that if she'd ever ripped you off."

"Chiana had more sense. She knew what I'd do if I ever caught her stealing from me."

"Once a Peacekeeper, always a Peacekeeper, huh, Aeryn?"

"And what's that supposed to mean?"

"Just that I think D'Argo's opinion of Peacekeeper morality may be right. It's rule through fear and intimidation, right?"

Aeryn stalked to her quarters and left Crichton to "riffle" through Chiana's things in peace. Later that evening, Zhaan convinced her to attend a ritual—The Pha-Lhokini, The Glad Return of Possessions.

Crichton had referred to the ceremony as "The Return of the Prodigal Purse," a reference that no doubt drew much from human culture, but which made absolutely no sense to Aeryn. Seated in a circle with the others, she was having mixed emotions. Would Crais have laughed at her? Feel she had wasted her Peacekeeper training and potential? Aeryn had given up trying to fathom the motivations of her former commander—indeed, her former culture. Exposure to these few so-called criminals had brought about some significant changes to her view of herself, her life, her beliefs.

According to Zhaan's explanation, the ceremony was to restore the items stolen by Chiana over the months she had been on Moya to their proper owners.

For some reason, this also had to be accompanied by much meaningful chanting.

As Crichton had put it, "Chiana ripped us off, and now we're ripping it right back."

For Zhaan, the ceremony held more symbolic and meaningful overtones. It was about acceptance, closure, healing. Normally, it would have been held for one departed never to return, if not actually dead, and would also have included the dispersal of personal possessions. This would have been symbolic of the spread of pollen, the seeding of new life. Alright, in this instance it seemed to have much more to do with the return of stolen goods. But then, that was Chiana for you. A wild and crazy girl, and one that they would miss, in their own ways.

Zhaan led the chanting, triggering a sceptical response from D'Argo and a frankly amused one from Crichton. Aeryn felt like a detached observer. She was sure Chiana had never dared steal anything from her. If she had . . . well, the little thief knew what Aeryn thought of criminals. Fortunately, Chiana realized who she was dealing with.

Chanting finally over, Zhaan moved to a large clay bowl, the traditional receptacle for diasporic possessions.

"First to emerge from the bowl of life," Zhaan intoned gently, "ELO—*Out of the Blue.*" Zhaan reverently handed the disc to Crichton. He took it with a broad grin.

"Hey, excellent. I wondered where that had gone. Hey, D'Argo, have you seen the spaceship on the cover of this album? Bet you wish you had a roadster like that, huh?"

D'Argo scowled. "I do not."

Zhaan continued, "Second to emerge from the bowl of life—a Peacekeeper stun rifle power pack."

Aeryn was clearly startled. "How did the little witch manage . . ." She broke off in sudden embarrassment. It wouldn't do to let everyone know how easily she had missed such an important item. She nodded her thanks as she took the power pack from Zhaan.

"Third to emerge, a Peacekeeper ID chip. Fourth to emerge, a Peacekeeper credit chip. Fifth to emerge, one pair of Peacekeeper regulation issue work boots."

By now everyone was howling with laughter.

But their merriment was cut short. Pilot's voice came over the comms. He tried to suppress his anxiety as he stated Moya's ever-deteriorating condition. Of course, he was also in pain—as one linked symbiotically with the dying ship, that was to be expected. Her joy was his—and her agony, too. It was not just the possibility of Pilot's death that Moya found so upsetting, but that the entire crew could also die. Unless they wanted to live on Jansz's ship, and under his control, it was unlikely they would find any refuge in the Uncharted Territories. Moya's liberators lived within her, and she was always concerned for their welfare. To know that they would die with her was a pain that pierced more deeply than any sickness.

With Moya, Pilot needed no words. Just the image of comfort to stave off the pain as long as possible. *They will help us soon. I promise.*

Between Moya and the trader fleet lay an area of dead space. An almost completely insignificant percentage of this space was now filled with a drifting field of refuse. A tiny portion of this galactic flotsam comprised two somewhat shell-shocked Hynerians.

Rygel and Nyaella drifted in zero-g within their newly acquired Lifebuoy, tethered to Rygel's ThroneSled, which was homing in slowly but surely on the living gravitational well that was Moya. Both Hynerians were giggling—an understandable reaction to the shock of their near-death and even narrower escape.

"Did you see . . ."

"The look on his face when . . ."

"They just went *pop* . . ."

Painful sighs. Rygel rubbed his aching ribs. He glanced out of the view port. They'd covered about half the distance from Jansz's flagship to Moya.

"How's the air supply?" Rygel asked Nyaella.

"According to the emergency manual it . . . oh! According to the manual it just ran out."

The laughter stopped.

A small light blinked on the diagnostics board.

"What's that, Nyaella?"

"Let's see." Nyaella thumbed through the pages of the manual. "It's a Peacekeeper emergency homing beacon."

Rygel groaned. All they needed now was for Crais or some other ill-intentioned Peacekeeper force to discover them.

With Moya ill they'd be perfect targets.

"Can't you switch it off?" Rygel demanded.

"I don't know. And I'd appreciate it if you wouldn't take that tone with me. You may be Dominar, but I am most definitely not a commoner."

"I'm sorry."

"So you should be."

"And I hope you realize what a privilege it is getting an apology from . . ." Rygel broke off, suddenly aware how ridiculous he sounded under the circumstances. "Nyaella, I'm a pompous old Dominar with delusions of grandeur and a crew of misfits for my empire."

Nyaella's expression softened. "You're still the Hynerian of my dreams."

She leaned closer to Rygel, her presence overpowering, inviting an act he had missed for so long he could barely remember it.

"No," his voice shook. "I can't. Not yet."

Her voice was sympathetic. "I understand."

"Do you?"

Rygel's voice was full of regret. Days and months and years of regret. And rather more self-pity. "Do you really? How could you? How could you understand? You're not a Dominar. You've never borne the weight, the burden of an empire, for so long . . . only to be cast aside after a lifetime's work like . . . like so much . . . unwanted furniture . . ."

"You weren't cast aside. You were deposed by your cousin Bishan."

Rygel groaned. "Tell that to my heart . . ." his voice caught and he broke off.

Nyaella studied him closely but said nothing.

Towed by the ThroneSled, the Lifebuoy moved closer to Moya. Its hyperwave emergency signal, transmitted on a broad-range Peacekeeper frequency, beamed steadily out into the Uncharted Territories. If the Lifebuoy had been facing in a slightly different direction, Rygel and Nyaella would have been able to see the apothecary shuttle that passed around the field of refuse, delicately avoiding the less choice items, careful to avoid the presence of contaminant upon the hull of the vessel that might have transferred to their sick, city-sized patient.

The shuttle entered Moya through her aft dorsal vent. White-suited apothecaries unpacked a large number of carefully sterilized crates. From the crates emerged several thousand small drones. Each was no larger than Crichton's hand, each contained a tiny antigrav drive, a simple target recognition and guidance system and a glass phial of culture medium. Growing on the bluish jelly, though invisible to the human eye, were several billion undifferentiated cell packets cloned from Moya's embryonic nucleus. Bonded to the cell culture was a smart-molecule comprising biological triggers devised following experimentation with the various components of Moya's genetic make-up.

Watching this activity, Crichton expressed an interest in the method of the cure. Eventually he was noticed by the assistant to the chief apothecary in residence, and graced with a brief explanation.

"The method is simple enough. The drones will deliver the T-cells to the sites of infection and damage; there the infected tissue will bond with the smart-molecule as part of its normal pathology. Once infected, the smart-molecule will read the composition of the necrotising virus, select the appropriate chemical trigger, load this into the T-Cell grouping as a viral packet and inject the whole lot into the site of infection. All you have to do then is wait while the infection runs its course and whatever organs damaged by the infection are re-grown. A brief period of observation and recuperation will follow, and then Moya will be restored to full health. If you have any questions, I'm sure the apothecary will be glad to answer them more fully—after the procedure."

The assistant cast a troubled glance at Crichton's bare hands and uncovered boots. "Now if you will excuse us, this is a Grade One controlled site and you have not been sterilized." And with that Crichton found himself unceremoniously bundled out of the chamber.

He wandered to the bridge to think. The apothecary's explanation seemed logical. But while the others were hopeful, Crichton felt more comfortable playing the pessimist—and waited for the inevitable fly in the ointment.

It wasn't long in arriving.

Vurid stood quivering at the side of his master as Lord Jansz perused with crawling eyes the interior of the cell that, until recently, had held a certain Hynerian royal.

"Tell me, Vurid, was I good to her? Did I love her?"

"Yes, Lord. Yes, Lord," Vurid assured his master.

"And these Moya individuals. Did I not trade fairly, and with honor?"

"Yes, Lord."

"And did I not observe protocol?"

"Yes, Lord."

"And even make allowances when the Hynerian . . . the puny Hynerian . . ." The voices subsided, dropping in volume and in frequency almost into the subsonic. "I will not have it, Vurid. To be exploited in this manner. To be the victim of such deceit and disrespect."

"Vurid agrees, Lord."

"An agreement was made and has now been broken."

"Vurid sympathizes, Lord."

"You were responsible for Nyaella, Vurid."

"Vurid admits this is true, Lord."

"Then Vurid will be dead—along with everyone else—*if Vurid does not get her back!*"

"Vurid understands, Lord."

"Order everyone into the boats. Make best speed to attack. And contact Moya's crew immediately. Protocol demands fair warning before destruction. We are not, after all, common murderers."

"Yes, Lord. At once, Lord. Vurid obeys."

The communication came as Moya was moving away from the nomad flotilla. In her weakened condition, she was unable to StarBurst. Instead, she had opted to move closer to the nearby blue supergiant star—as Pilot said, "Moya likes the warmth."

Crichton winced at Pilot's words. "Pilot, you can tell Moya from me she picked a hell of a comforter."

"I will be sure to pass on your sentiments."

According to instrument readings, the blue supergiant was currently emitting radiation levels that would be capable of eradicating all life on Earth in a matter of hours.

Moya had reached a distance of three astronomical units from the fleet—some half the distance to the ambit of the supergiant—when the viewtank buzzed and clicked, and scattered static into the field of view. A moment, then a familiar face shuddered into existence. Judging by his tone of voice, and the single tear scorching a fresh scar into his steel collar, today had not been a good day for Trader-Prime Jansz.

"Give her back or you will be destroyed." The Free-Trader's four voices pulsed like recently serviced machinery. Crichton tried not to let himself dwell on the thought that, whatever it was that had ticked Jansz off, the Trader-Prime thought enough of the matter to present himself in person, as an individual, rather than through his gestalt Compound.

Crichton looked around the bridge. Zhaan, D'Argo, and Aeryn were equally puzzled.

"Give who back?" Crichton was clearly exasperated. He pinched the bridge of his nose with a thumb and forefinger. A tension headache was building up behind his eyes. What he wouldn't give for a couple of aspirin. Or a generous shot of Scotch.

"The Lady Skitrovex. Nyaella Skitrovex." Jansz's main voice shifted; the harmony was now rounded and pleasant.

"Nyaella Skitrovex?" Crichton repeated dumbly.

"The royal Hynerienne. And do not talk so loudly. Your voice is painful to one's sensitive ears." Was he serious? The ears in question resembled jet exhausts.

Aeryn frowned, thick brows clenching over furious eyes. "I'd say we all know what that means."

A general light of understanding spread around the bridge. Understanding . . . and anger.

"Jansz. Hang fire, we'll be right back at you. Pilot, cut transmission." Crichton flushed angrily. "Rygel. Where is he? I told him . . . I warned him what would happen if he let his mivonks do his thinking."

On the bridge, Pilot announced mournfully, "I am afraid there's more bad news."

The viewtank image swirled and reformed as an exterior view. Backlit by the heart-rendingly familiar spiral nebula, Jansz's flagship was a dense shadow bristling with gun ports, as stark and uncompromising an example of a man o' war as was ever seen or imagined by man. Gaping like mouths, the gun ports promised lethal kisses. Ranged about the man o' war were two or three dozen skiffs. All had one design configuration in common.

Trying to count the open gun ports, Crichton thought, could make a man cross-eyed.

Seeing the expression on Crichton's face, undoubtedly sensing the coming storm, Zhaan voiced her opinion with quiet desperation. "John, remember the First Principle. Mediate between your inner and outer selves . . . let go of your anger . . ."

"Oh I'll let it go alright. S.I.G., Cap'n Blue. Pilot, where's Rygel? The little slimebag! I'm going to rip him apart—if either of us lives long enough."

Crichton sprinted to Rygel's quarters. Rygel turned as Crichton entered, favoring the human with a contemptuous look.

"Don't humans know how to knock?" the Hynerian had the nerve to ask.

"Guess why I'm smiling, Sparky," Crichton said through gritted teeth.

"I have no idea."

"Because I'm pleased t'see ya."

"Hmnph. Not convinced. Was a time when I didn't have to put up with such overt familiarity. Was a time when I was surrounded by art. Beautiful things, beautiful females . . . thousands of beautiful females . . ."

"Y'know what they say. It's quality, not quantity, that counts."

"So you say. I have my own ideas."

"Oh. You have ideas?"

"Yes, I do. Big ideas."

Rygel watched with apprehension as the enormous human moved closer.

Crichton walked his fingers across Rygel's leathery head, "Really? Big ideas—and in such a small head."

There was no getting away from the human. His strong fingers had closed, pincer-firm around Rygel's ear.

"Big ideas such as kidnap? Big ideas such as getting laid? Big ideas such as *getting us all killed?!*" Crichton punctuated each question with a slap. The last slap sent the Hynerian swaying, a slippery pendulum in Crichton's grip. Rygel spluttered a few of his favorite obscenities.

Crichton tipped his head to one side and considered. "Aw, you don't think you're being shown the proper respect? I'm not dissing you, am I? You don't think that, do you, Rygel?"

Rygel struggled to look dignified. "You're here on my sufferance, Crichton," he said in his most condescending tone. "Now why don't you just say what you've come here to say and leave me alone?"

Crichton tightened his grip. The one-time leader of six hundred billion souls yelped indignantly as he was nearly lifted from his seat.

"Crichton," Rygel implored, "what do you want?"

"Sparky, ol' pal, ol' bean. The time has come. We need you."

"Need me?" His voice ballooned with self-importance. "Naturally you need me." The limbs suddenly froze. "Why do you need me?"

"Because you have negotiation skills."

"Negotiation skills. Yes, indeed, I do. In fact, in my younger days I was considered to be quite the . . ." Rygel paused. He was distinctly uneasy. "Uh, negotiation with whom, precisely? And for what?"

"With Free-Trader Jansz, that's precisely with whom. And for what? For our lives, Sparky, our lives!" Crichton's shouted reply made Rygel's head throb.

Crichton hummed "Rubber Bullets" as he dragged Rygel out of his quarters and through Moya's port-tertiary artery towards the bridge.

"Listen to me, Crichton. I'm warning you. I won't be bullied like this."

"Bullied? My small green friend, you have no idea what a world of hurt you're in."

"Hurt?" Rygel's voice quavered apprehensively. "You mean . . . actual pain?" A nervous laugh. "Well then, in that case—I can be reasonable."

"Oh, we're way past reasonable. We're so far past reasonable it hurts. Wanna know why? Trader-Prime Jansz wants to kill us. Chiana's got her finger on the trigger. Zhaan says we should neuter you—just for your own enlightenment, you understand—and I wouldn't be surprised if D'Argo takes a blunt knife and cuts off your . . ."

"Ooh! Really? Cut off my—? They're that angry? Oh, but you'd stop them, wouldn't you Crichton? You wouldn't let them do that to me? I mean, you said yourself, it's not as if we're not *friends*."

"Friends. Hmm. Let me see. Would a *friend* risk the

lives of his companions by running off with the girl-
friend and cash cow of the only being who could save
Moya's life? Oh, you know what?" Crichton's dangerously mild tone cranked itself up to a frightening
shout. "I don't think so, Rygel!"

Rygel shivered at the concussion of sound. Everything about the human was just too big. Except its
brain, apparently.

"I haven't—I mean, I, I—didn't . . . that is . . . it's
not as if she . . . as if we . . ." Skin slapped wetly
against skin. If only the wretched greebol could stretch
his achingly alien brain enough to understand. Understand what Nyaella Skitrovex meant to the royal line,
what she meant to him.

"Tell me where you stashed her, Sparky."

"I don't know what you . . ."

Crichton twisted Rygel's ear.

"She's in the cargo bay subsidiary nutrient artery."

"Rygel, that's the most sensible reply you've made
all week. Now listen carefully. I want you to go to the
bridge. Get on the horn to Jansz and make your apolo-
gies. Tell him you're going to let him have the princess
back. Do it before he brings his big guns to bear and
blasts the lot of us to Kingdom Come. Not going too
fast for you am I, sport?"

Rygel sniffed indignantly at the stupidity of humans. His courage rose as his fear drained away.
"Crichton, do you have any idea how much Nyaella is
worth to the royal family? As long as she's aboard,
Jansz will never attack. If she dies, his ransom goes up
in smoke as well. It's all trader bluff. Trust me on
this—I'm a politician. We're all perfectly safe."

Moya seemed to shudder. The artery through which Crichton was dragging Rygel convulsed and contracted. The ceiling lowered, the floor rose and the walls shook with spasmodic shock waves the size of desert sand dunes. Human and Hynerian found themselves tumbling painfully along the skinsteel floor.

Pilot's voice came over Crichton's comm.

"A preemptive attack. Trader Jansz has apparently lost patience with negotiation."

"'Trust me, I'm a politician.'" Crichton muttered furiously. "Must remember that one. I'm sure it'll be a great deal of use—when we're all blown to bits!"

Another explosion blasted Crichton off his feet. Rygel slammed into the skinsteel wall. Flame belched along the corridor, closely followed by the smell of barbecued starship.

Valve-muscles contracted. The artery pinched shut on either side of them. Crichton scrambled to his feet. Light from nearby clumps of lumoss, normally an even shade of pearl, was now strobing wildly across a wild spectrum.

"Rygel?" Crichton finally gathered his addled wits enough to check for something even more obvious. "Hey! Sparky, you with me?"

No answer.

The lights went out in a flicker of indigo fireworks.

Crichton looked around. In the swiftly gathering gloom he could just make out Rygel's ThroneSled projecting from the distant artery valve—crushed almost flat by the skinsteel seam. There was blood on the dented stabilizer fins. Rygel was nowhere to be seen. At least, his body was nowhere to be seen.

His ear, however, was plainly visible, lying in a small puddle of blood beside the smashed chair.

CHAPTER 6

Moya convulsed in pain as another blast tore into her hull. She was overwhelmed with fear and desperate to escape. Too weak to StarBurst to safety, she was a helpless target as Jansz's gun skiffs took up position, swarming like insects around her, their gun ports wide open and belching fire.

As a child, Crichton had read science fiction. Now he was living it, and the fact was that space was a much simpler place than anyone had previously imagined. There were, though, a few basic rules of thumb.

Anything you get wrong could kill you.

Anything you forget could kill you.

When in doubt, assume anything can kill you.

Simple, and easy to remember. Especially when seated in *Farscape I* and facing dozens of heavily armed gun skiffs crewed by ruthless killers. He wondered if the ramshackle armaments system that he and Aeryn had hastily cobbled together and mounted on

Farscape I would even survive takeoff, let alone a vicious dogfight.

"Well, I'll soon find out," Crichton muttered to himself. He squared his shoulders and steeled himself for battle. He was resolved to go out and give as good an account of himself as he could.

As a child, he'd read books in which interstellar war consisted of anything from two pilots marooned on a barren world, with nothing but a pocket knife and their wit with which to fight, to gargantuan fleets of glittering starships with gravity rays so powerful they could smash planets together like so many snooker balls. The reality, as with everything else in life, was much simpler.

When in doubt, assume anything can kill you. Because when anything you do may kill you, you've got nothing to lose. And a man with nothing to lose has a chance of winning.

At least that's what he kept telling himself as he pushed forward on the powerboost and flew *Farscape I* out of Moya's cargo bay on a tail of cold fire, with death in his eyes and a scream in his heart.

He didn't feel like an imperiled pilot. He felt like a kid on a go-cart, shooting concrete rapids and giving fate the finger.

There were days when you needed a good scrap.

Aeryn studied the battle readouts on the heads-up display. Her Prowler was the most perfect Peacekeeper design, a marriage of technology and inspiration that had been with her since before she could walk. It listened and saw for her, projecting its prodigious observations and lightning conclusions via laser beam directly onto her retinal implants. It was her sister. Her twin. Panther-black and built for murder.

When she was in her Prowler, Aeryn Sun was in love. The universe was her mother, the cold alloy hull her father, the targeting and weapons systems her beloved family. She was complete.

Calm.

Cold.

Perfect.

Aeryn remained motionless, cupped in black alloy, held tight against the rip and shear of g-force, temperature even. She did not sweat. She existed merely as an adjunct to the whole, definable only by its blinding speed and constantly evolving angular vectors. The sum of its parts, its motion, its momentum, and its pilot, she whizzed through the air—now here, now there—quicker than sight, faster than thought. A precise vector, a minimal command to the weapons systems: Tiny suns were born in cold metal, hot reactors; hull alloy split, and bloomed into the barren void.

A heartbeat.

Target, fire, avoid, alter vector, target, fire, so—

Aeryn sped like lightning.

And she felt nothing.

Crichton fed Blue Oyster Cult into the sound system of *Farscape 1* and primed the weapons pod upgrades, praying that they wouldn't let him down. "Don't Fear the Reaper" kicked in and he stamped on the afterburners. Flame belched from bell nozzles. His face pressed tight against his skull, eyes wide, gaze fixed on target star after target star as each swung through his flattened field of vision.

Crichton's hand gripped the powerboost, hammered the firing grip. His body shook with his ship as the guns warped space. Somewhere nearby an alloy flower bloomed and lives were snuffed out in the cold vacuum.

The Prowler flew, coughed flame and spacewarps, blasted hulls and lives to molecular dust. Four ships fell to her guns, five, six, ten. Still they came. Eleven ships, twelve, fifteen. She fired to kill—and her laser-accurate eyes were keen.

Corpses of gun skiffs littered space, drifting; precise holes punched through their weapons and drive systems.

This was war.

Kill or be killed.

Anything else was simply not efficient.

By the time Blue Oyster Cult had reached the second chorus of "Don't Fear the Reaper," Crichton had disabled or destroyed three skiffs. Seven more homed in on his exhaust while the remaining dozen or so ships vectored on Moya, her galleon flanks pulsing with rainbow fire as she moved away from the conflict as best she could. Moya had to ride out the storm—Crichton and Aeryn had to try to minimize that storm.

Proximity alarms blared—seven marks vectoring in, metal wasps with sunfire for stingers. Crichton could feel the target sights closing around his neck. A dull ache throbbed at the back of his head, but it was a pain that adrenaline flushed aside. Later he would pay, but for now he needed to be clear. Clear and focused.

Crichton lined up a shot; his weapons' pulse took out the lead ship. A second salvo fused the engines on a nearby attacker to slag. A third had two ships colliding as fuel exploded in a spectacular display of light.

A Peacekeeper acolyte might have studied Crichton's black box recorder and shaken her head in amazement. Crichton was slow. Crichton was inaccurate. Crichton was singing. But Crichton had one thing on his side. He was lucky.

Four ships down.

Stars became blurred arcs.

Fire rained in molten streams.

But no luck lasts forever.

Three ships closed in, vectoring on his exhaust, loosing flame that slathered across the void, licked hungrily about *Farscape*'s hull. Crichton knew that unless he could get behind and above his pursuers he was doomed. He swooped around to his right in a sudden loop, but the ships remained glued to his tail. He dipped and zigzagged, trying somehow to shake them, managing to avoid the deadly fire they unleashed, but they followed his every move remorselessly, relentlessly. And they were gaining ground, getting that little bit closer to him with his every desperate maneuver.

In his peripheral vision, he saw Aeryn's Prowler to his left, wreaking havoc. She was his only chance. If he could fly directly in front of her . . . If his pursuers remained locked in pursuit, oblivious to anything else . . . If Aeryn recognized *Farscape I* and didn't shoot him down . . . If she could make mincemeat of all three of the ships on his tail . . . he might make it.

There were a lot of ifs, but this chance was all he had. He dipped a little and swept around, tracing a wide arc, and headed in her direction.

Crippled, traumatized, Moya fell towards the blue star.

Azure radiance warmed her, bathed the carbonized wounds the Trader weapons had carved into her flanks and belly. For now, the warmth was a comfort—but soon it would spell her death. Pain lashed her, sparked and fumed within her body. Parts of her burned slowly, bleeding, flaming gouts of air and flesh, instantly snuffed out in the vacuum. Weak and imbalanced hormonally from the recent necrosis, her mind recoiled from the attack, seeking refuge in other places, more comforting times.

She was travelling backwards. Falling through her own memories. Running from Leviathan Hunters. Hiding in the shadows of moons. Discovery. Slavery. The control collar. The prisoners.

She remembered her pod, swimming together through an ocean of stars. She recalled playing in the detritus of a moon, hide-and-seek among the ruin-rings. She remembered her first mate-pair. So long ago, yet still so clear.

Memories coded into her DNA brought Moya a vision of her own birth. Her parents, hunted through the last arns of their lives. The adults of the pod sacrificing their own lives to preserve hers, until finally only her mother remained, straining with the child Moya, too full to StarBurst, hounded by Leviathan Hunters, to the edge of the Black Nebula.

Conceived in starlight, the child Moya had been born in the icy corpse of a solar system. Already an orphan at the moment of birth, her first awareness had been of dizzying flight, of starstorm and black sucking horror.

Her mother had been clever. Hunted, and knowing escape was impossible, the adult Leviathan had headed for the very edge of the most dangerous of stellar phenomena. A black hole. Those ships foolish enough to follow her too closely perished, shredded by gravitational forces.

The rest of the Leviathan Hunter fleet remained beyond the event horizon, waiting. The adult had served her purpose. For her, there would be no escape, and her child would be theirs from birth, the first Leviathan to be born in captivity, the first of a new slave-species. This one, the Leviathan Hunters were sure, would not be born free.

Determined to save her child, Moya's mother had chosen to give birth at the edge of the known universe, the place where time and space gave way to forces unknown. Here she gave new life to the universe and here her own life ended, sacrificed in exchange for a precisely calculated orbital vector for her newborn daughter. Her body fell where not even light could escape. Three Leviathan Hunters followed her there, splashed around the event horizon, a dark corona, invisible beacon of her birth. And in the moments before dissolution, Moya burst from her mother and accelerated away.

The adult Leviathan surrendered Moya to a lightless, violent, and greedy part of the universe. Old beyond measure, the ravenous maw had sucked matter and light from the universe for millennia; mercilessly eviscerating its galactic prey and swallowing the tidal entrails. Moya fell into its grip for moments only but in that time centuries passed in the universe, according to immutable relativistic law.

The Leviathan Hunters left in search of easier prey, sired children of their own, grew old, and died. Moya moved fractions of a degree of arc, cleaved from the universe in which she had been born, a frozen image if any could have seen her.

While Moya experienced her first confused thought: *I'm falling.*

the sons and daughters of the Leviathan Hunters who had hunted her became families, generations— and a new culture emerged into the light of older suns.

Moya blinked and Earth's Stone Age lived and died. Her heartbeats drummed throughout the Bronze Age, the Iron Age, the age of the microchip, the age of space flight.

Moya breathed.

A rural world blackened with industrialization became cluttered with orbital junk.

Moya breathed.

An already technologically advanced culture reached far into the galaxy.

The child Moya emerged eventually from the event horizon to her first experience of nonrelativistic time. Her playthings then were moons and her secret places the halos of stars. Her mother's sacrifice had not been in vain. Moya was born free.

Slowly, the painful memory of her mother and her birth faded, subsumed in the wonder and fear that was life in this new universe that was now her home. But no luck lasts forever.

Moya lived for a space of time that, for human culture, brought five returns of a comet named Halley, before thinking to seek out others like herself and learn a fearful truth.

For the Peacekeepers, Leviathans had become beasts of burden. Shackled and collared, they had for generations provided a ready source of living space; upgraded with technology they had become programmable, multipurpose, intelligent tools. Transport, shipping, colonizing, terraforming, all these tasks could be performed by one such as Moya—at minimal cost and for enormous profit.

Moya shuddered as the memories brought greater pain than even her wounds. Then the memory shattered, replaced by a dying solar system bathed in blue light. Rainbow fire lapped at her flesh, shocking Moya back to the present. And a new realization.

She had been born falling around a dead star. Now Moya found herself falling again, towards the savage azure furnace that was the dying supergiant, and perhaps to her death. With her fell a smattering of flotsam, insignificant blobs of alloy and organic life tumbling in her smouldering gravitational wake.

Death was close.

Crichton could feel the ships behind him, could almost feel the crosshairs on their gun sights lock on to him. He dipped the craft again, and three blasts raced harmlessly overhead. He was still alive. But for how much longer?

Suddenly, sparks flew from the instrument panel and Blue Oyster Cult abruptly ended. At the same moment, he saw one of the forward-mounted guns come loose from its mountings and bang against the fuselage, dangling uselessly from a web of wiring.

"Cowboy contractors," he had time to mutter before he realized that he was losing power. He frantically shoved and pulled at the powerboost, but there was no response. He was falling through space.

Then he saw Aeryn's Prowler turn towards him. He prayed that she recognized him. The Prowler was black as night, visible only because of the hole it cut in the stars. It was a superb machine. A real class act. And speaking of Aeryn, she was pretty much a class act herself, thought Crichton, watching her with admiration her as she methodically took out his pursuers.

Three metal deathflowers bloomed, and the gun skiffs that had followed him were gone. It was as simple as that.

But his sense of relief was short-lived. The remaining weapons pod on Crichton's hull suddenly ripped apart and fell away. He watched it drift past, trailing wires, looking like some metallic squid. He wondered if the entire craft was about to break up. It didn't look like it. In fact, it all seemed sound.

Defenseless, Crichton felt a strange sense of calm. There wasn't much he could do now. He was no longer in control of his own destiny. He would just drift until someone shot him down. He just wished the sound system hadn't packed up on him. He thought about ejecting. But ejecting into what? Space? Ejecting was just suicide by another name. Better just to drift in *Farscape*.

He allowed himself to daydream. He was a kid again, sinking down in the big, deep sofa, staying up to watch *The Six Million Dollar Man*. Mangled in an experimental re-entry vehicle wreck, Steve Austin had been put back together again with high-tech bionic implants in his arms and legs. He could run at sixty kph. He could punch a hole in a brick wall. He could pull over a light aircraft.

As a kid, Crichton had wondered how the guy managed to do that stuff without ripping his arms and legs clear off his body. Maybe the limbs could handle the force applied, but the body would never have been able to take it.

But, hey, Steve Austin was cool.

Maybe whoever found him after he crashed would be able to put him together again—a space age Humpty Dumpty. He'd be able to armwrestle two-hundred-kilo gorillas. And win. Now that would be cool.

Then something interrupted his daydream—it was his comm. Something in his module was working. Maybe he shouldn't write himself off just yet. Crichton straightened up, instantly alert.

"Crichton, what's the matter with you? We have a job to do. This is no time to go walkabout!"

"Aeryn?" he responded, tentatively.

"Who else?" came the terse reply.

"No one," Crichton answered. "I was just surprised to hear from you. I didn't think anything was working in here."

"You've got problems?"

"You could say that."

"Status?"

"Up shit creek without a paddle probably covers it."

"Clarify."

"The weapons upgrades both tore loose and I lost power. I guess something must have shorted."

"Have you tried restarting the engine?"

"No." *How dumb can you be?*

"Then do it. Come on. I've disabled a number of their ships but more have launched on an intercept vector. We have to get back to Moya."

Crichton pushed the powerboost. Nothing happened.

"Nothing," he said.

"Try again."

"Easy for you to say," Crichton muttered through gritted teeth. He wrestled with the powerboost and reset all the instruments. "Nothing, nada, niente," he said finally.

"OK, I get the picture. Eject and I'll pick you up."

And then—a miracle.

His port engine caught.

"Wait, I've got something. I've got power again," Crichton shouted, hardly believing his luck.

"OK. Now we head back to Moya."

"Hold on. Where is Moya? I only have one engine. And I'm defenseless. I'll never make it."

"You've got to."

Crichton saw them before she did. Two gun skiffs heading their way. And they had more than simply passing the time of day on their minds, judging by their open gun ports.

"Uh-oh," he said. "We've got company."

There was a short pause while Aeryn assessed the situation.

"I'll take them. You just try to keep yourself out of trouble."

"Wilco."

"What?"

"I'll try to do that."

Then Aeryn was gone and Crichton was left to wrestle with his crippled craft. He wondered if the problem with the starboard engine was caused by the gun that hadn't fallen free. If he could dislodge it and its cat's cradle of wires, he might be able to restart that engine, too. He rocked *Farscape I* gently up and down but the gun stubbornly refused to budge. He'd have to land somewhere and rip it free.

Keeping the ship on a steady course with only one working engine was not an easy operation and he zigzagged wildly through the sky. Behind him, the sky lit up briefly, twice. Aeryn had completed her latest mission. He waited for her to join him again.

Aeryn didn't want John Crichton to die. She liked the feeling of being an individual, to think for herself, set her own goals, choose her own friends—maybe even to love and be loved. All things she'd learned from this strange human. No, Aeryn most definitely did not want John Crichton to die.

She knew these feelings were important, but she didn't know where they would take her. There was much she didn't understand. There was so much about her that seemed to puzzle or in some way offend the man—the alien—to whom she felt such a strong, but confusing, bond. And there was so much about him that confused and even angered her.

Why did she feel such an overwhelming need to be understood by him anyway? Growing up in the Peacekeeper world, only the group, not the individual, was important. The whole was, after all, stronger than its parts. Hadn't it always been so?

How else could order be maintained? Total support for the chosen enforcers of laws—that was the only way. And since everyone was a potential criminal, the

Peacekeepers were necessary—they gave their lives to
ensure compliance with all the countless rules and reg-
ulations. Hadn't it been a perfect system? But, then,
what had gone wrong? How had the culture that had
trained her, become corrupt?

Less than a cycle ago, Aeryn Sun had been part of unit
05 in tactical squadron 4, one of eight highly trained
peace enforcement officers whose job had been to up-
hold the law and protect the innocent. Programmed
from birth for perfection, for purity, for the pursuit of
whatever aims and goals her culture dictated, Aeryn
had flown almost before she could walk, cradled in her
Prowler. She had trained before puberty with Peacekeeper energy weapons, had eaten, breathed and
dreamed Peacekeeper tactics and Peacekeeper law. In
short, she had been raised and schooled to be the perfect officer and the perfect warrior.

But now Aeryn was no longer just a cog in a machine. She was a Sebacean, a woman, and an individual—and she saw no reason why she should be judged
by the standards of her culture any more. She wanted
to be judged on her own merits. As an individual. As
Aeryn Sun.

This was what she liked about Crichton. He didn't
judge. He watched, he learned, and he considered. He
valued. And in return he was valued. Human culture
was strange, alien, and in many ways disturbing. But it
was also desirable. No, she didn't want Crichton to
die. Not now or ever.

These thoughts flashed through Aeryn's mind as she
turned her Prowler away from the gun skiffs she had
destroyed and sought out Crichton again.

When she saw his craft, limping haphazardly through space, a strange feeling of warmth welled up inside her, and she flew her ship to the side of his.

"So," she asked, "how's it going?"

"I really need to put down to make some running repairs."

"Yes," Aeryn acknowledged, "but where?"

"I'm open to suggestions," he said and she thought she heard him laugh.

"Well, there is a place and it's not somewhere that Jansz and his bunch of pirates would expect us to land. But it is a little crazy."

"I'll take crazy at the moment. Where do you have in mind?"

"Jansz's Compound," came the reply.

There was a long silence.

"Crichton," Aeryn queried, "you still there?"

"Yeah, I'm still here."

"And?"

"You're right. That is crazy. I'll be blasted out of the sky before I'm even close."

"You are close. Look. It's just over there. And there's no one there to blast you out of the sky. All the gun skiffs are long gone, heading towards Moya. Anyway, I'll be with you. My Prowler can take care of any attackers."

Crichton knew that was true. He regarded the huge craft. The vast flight deck was open and empty. No way could Crichton miss it, even with one engine. And they did have a chance—a wafer-thin chance—that they could land, repair *Farscape I,* and take off again without being spotted. And if they were spotted? Well, at least they would still be alive, and, as she was sure

Crichton would say, if she gave him the opportunity, where there's life, there's hope.

"Why is it that there's never a good malt whisky to hand when you most need it?"

"I don't know, Crichton. Why is that?"

"OK," he said, "I'll try it. But you stay well away. I'm going in alone."

"Oh no, Crichton. You're defenseless. I'm coming, too. And there isn't anything you can do about it."

This time the silence was so lengthy that she thought that he had cut the connection. Then his voice, crisp and authoritative, cut in.

"OK, Aeryn."

Inside Moya the temperature was rising. Skinsteel shivered: hot flushes. Alloy muscles contracted, groaning across escarpment bones. On the bridge, Zhaan and D'Argo were watching the viewtank. In the tank were eight models, neat as any child's toy: trader gun skiffs. Aggressive behavior long since curbed, all these pilots wanted now was to escape from their fiery tomb. But their ships were in trouble. Hungry claws of flame and gravity were reaching out from the blue star . . . reaching out to grasp, to hold and rend.

Screams came from the ships.

Tiny blossoms of light.

One by one the gun skiffs winked out of the universe, scattered to the solar winds.

Gradually the screams stopped, stepping down in increments until there was only the dreadful banshee wail of the supergiant to scar the reception wavelengths.

A witness to the unfolding drama, the behavior of

the bridge's occupants could not have been more different.

D'Argo paced, fists clenched impotently, lips set in a scowl prompted by his inability to affect the situation in any way. Zhaan stood quite still, eyes wide, skin tingling at the proximity of the erratically radiant supergiant. Agitation and calm, they were like two sides of the same coin. Storm and eye. As usual, D'Argo and Zhaan were arguing.

"You can't just blame Crichton." Zhaan. Voice of moderation. "Rygel is responsible in part."

"You are right. Rygel and Crichton are both to blame. They should both be killed."

"You're serious?"

"You must admit life would be far less complicated without them."

"I admit nothing. And you, D'Argo, must learn to moderate these extreme tendencies. What kind of world would it be if we killed everyone who ever annoyed us?"

"A happy one."

Zhaan sighed. "You'd be bored if you were happy."

"One day you will understand. One day someone will hurt you as deeply as I have been hurt. Then you will know in your heart that I am right, that all who behave dishonorably should perish."

"You think I know nothing of dishonor? Then, Ka D'Argo you do not understand what it is like to take a life."

"I am not a murderer if that is what you mean," D'Argo said with mounting anger.

"That is not what I meant." Zhaan, exasperated,

tried to ignore the effect the solar radiation was having on her body.

"Then why did you say it?" D'Argo snapped, temper roused, cheeks flushed. "Did you hope to improve my last minutes before we fall into that sun and our bodies are reduced to radioactive ashes."

"I . . ."

"Rygel needs help." Weary but still imperious, the voice heralded the arrival on the bridge of a curious duo. "I've done all I can for him."

"Rygel!"

Battered, bloody, scalp lacerated, face bruised, one ear torn clean off, head swathed in a bolt of royal purple cloth, the Hynerian Dominar languished in the arms of an unfamiliar figure. A Hynerienne. It had to be Nyaella.

"He says you're his friends. I'd be very grateful for your help. Before I drop him."

D'Argo's massive skull swiveled, his eyes targeting the new arrivals. "At last," the Luxan warrior pronounced, with a voice like thunder and a grateful glance at the wounded Dominar. "Someone to kill."

CHAPTER 7

It was ironic that it should be Chiana who saw the two crafts approaching the flight deck. She was investigating her new home, checking it out, exploring its possibilities.

Taking advantage of the fact that no one was bothered about her in the excitement, tension, and heightened activity of the attack on Moya. She was looking at what Jansz's world could offer an enterprising thief such as herself.

Chiana recognized Aeryn's Prowler and the limping *Farscape I* immediately and she wondered at the breathtaking audacity of Aeryn and Crichton bringing the battle to Jansz. Then she realized that they weren't attacking and wondered what they were up to. It didn't really matter. Whatever it was, they couldn't possibly get away with it. Or could they?

Most of the mechanics and support crew were distracted. No one seemed to notice the new arrivals.

Chiana watched as Crichton clambered out of his craft and busied himself at her hull. Aeryn soon joined him. Repairs, Chiana suddenly realized. Emergency repairs.

No one had yet challenged them. She smiled as she thought how close they were to success. If they could work speedily, and finish before anyone became suspicious, they might just make it.

But what did their lives mean to her? All she had ever wanted was to be happy. Happy and rich. Well, perhaps famous as well. But being rich was a condition she sought with all of her scheming mind and liar's heart.

It hadn't always been like that. She had started out with hope. The hope that no matter what sleazy frontier town life washed her into, no matter what lonely or desperate or perverse pleasures she had to indulge in to get by, maybe the next day would bring something brighter, a new chance. But the simple truth, even apparent to the younger Chiana, whose innocence she now only dimly remembered, was that, for her, there would be no bright tomorrow. Unless she stole one.

She peered at Aeryn and Crichton from her hiding place behind a pile of discarded engine parts. Crichton was completely absorbed in the repairs on *Farscape*. Aeryn was looking warily around, checking that they hadn't been discovered. Chiana knew that she would give them up in a heartbeat if the reward was sufficient.

Chiana's bright tomorrow had never come. In recent cycles she had even begun to acknowledge the growing truth that, for the woman she now was, it might not be enough if it did. To be happy and hopeful was not enough. To be contented. To be beautiful. To be loved. Not enough!

In all the universe, why had anyone ever thought these things important? She did not understand. Her parents, her so-called friends, everyone to whom she might have been important came, sooner or later, to regard her as a thing to be possessed, a trophy to be won, spoils of the social warfare others called love.

Her first theft had been passage off-world, away from the place of her birth, away from the suffocating love of others. And after that the stars beckoned, brighter than any trinkets, brighter even than jewels or gold, and the young Chiana could not resist their call. From the first moment when the commodities freighter on which she fled approached the world light years away from her home planet, Chiana knew that the stars were her friends. They were beacons, calling her to worlds just waiting for someone as talented, beautiful, amoral, and quick to learn as she.

So she had grown, choosing to avoid much contact with other beings, drifting from world to world, paying for passage with dirty favors, stealing what she could when she could. Gradually, as she grew older, she found herself equipped to deal easily with the worlds through which she passed. She was beautiful and she was intelligent. And she was possessed of a mysterious air that most men found irresistible.

Chiana had conned and thieved her way across sixty-eight solar systems. Far from the world of her birth, further and further into the darkness of the universe known only as the Uncharted Territories. Well, Chiana had charted them. With a ready smile and nimble fingers, she had moved, a white ghost among the immensity of stars. And Chiana had become very good at what she did.

Then she had met another mark. His name had been Halpern Frahn. He was a merchant banker, tall, handsome, rich, and gullible. The perfect subject. But something had happened, something unexpected, something she had never experienced before. By the time she realized she was in love, it was too late. She was the richest woman in four solar systems.

But Halpern Frahn was dead. The memory hardened her heart and galvanized her into action.

She left her hiding place silently and swiftly.

It was inevitable that it would be Chiana who betrayed Aeryn Sun and John Crichton. The sense of unease that she felt afterwards was, however, something very new.

A little over an arn later, Chiana joined the returning pilots of the gun skiffs on the quarterdeck. She felt her new shipmates drinking her in, mulling her over.

Fear, suspicion, judgement. She felt it coming off them in waves, like heat from a sun-baked desert.

She was the alien here.

She had a sudden flash . . .

Crichton had been talking about a book he had once read. *"So there's this guy, right, and he's called Valentine Michael Smith, and he's the first human born on another world, right? So they bring him home, to Earth, for the first time and he's never seen a human before and—well, the book's all about this guy learning about human culture, but it's also about us learn-*

ing about ourselves through the eyes of a stranger and—hmm. I guess you don't dig."

"Dig?"

"Understand. Relate. It's me. I mean, I'm him. The stranger. And you, all of you here on Moya, you're all my strange land . . ."

. . . of the way Crichton must have felt when he first arrived in the Uncharted Territories. Insecure. Afraid. Curious.

It had been a long time since she had known how it was to feel this way. Yet she could remember a time when these emotions were second nature to her. When every day brought a new danger to face or run from. How easily they had slipped from her, like old clothes, during the last few months.

Oh, the time spent on Moya had been a headlong dash from one life-threatening crisis to another. Or so it had seemed at the time. Standing now on the quarterdeck with the other pilots, Chiana began, for the first time, to understand that the truth had been very different. She hadn't realized what a comfort living on Moya had been.

Never having to look over your shoulder for fear of attack or abuse.

Never having to worry about where the next meal would come from, or if it would be poisonous.

The luxury of private quarters.

Time and space to think.

Company.

Comrades. Friends.

All gone now.

Vurid headed up the debriefing—interrupted by Jansz,

who continued his volcanic fit of rage by calling to task the pilot responsible for letting Moya and Nyaella Skitrovex escape.

The pilot was young, a fool, and would suffer. Chiana kept her eyes fixed on the ground. An old lesson, learned young and learned well. Be small. Be silent. Be invisible. Strange how easily she slipped back into the old ways.

The scene was played out with dreadful speed.

Anger evident in a furious minor ninth overtone to his vocal harmonic root, Jansz began, "Your name is Sciorrcco."

The terrified pilot's voice shook so hard his long incisors rattled.

"Speak."

"Yes. Yes, Lord Jansz."

"And do you understand why you have been called to task?"

"I, I, I . . ."

Jansz sighed; wind howling through canyons. "You were responsible for the Lady Skitrovex's rescue squadron."

"Ye-yes, sir, but . . ."

"No buts, please. Your position was an important one. A reward for many cycles spent dedicated to my service."

"Yes, Lord. It was. But if I might explain . . ."

"You may not." Soft. Baritone whisper with choral harmonic overtones. "You may, however, have full permission to pay for your mistake."

"Mistake? But I . . ."

"Do you have the Lady Skitrovex? Perhaps you

have secreted her about your person? Somewhere we are not able to see?"

"No, of course not, but—the Leviathan, Lord—it fell in, into the, the—sun and . . ."

"No excuses." A dismissive solo. "Vurid."

"Lord."

"Administer demonstrative punishment. Ten lashes."

"Immediately, Lord."

Chiana blinked. The Facilitator moved, forward and back, stinger a deadly whip through air and skin and muscle.

Sciorrcco shuddered, his body annihilating itself as the neurotoxin spread through his bloodstream, mouth wide, voice unwinding from a shriek to a scream, a cry, a whisper. The stinger lashed again and again. As muscles wound tighter tendons split and bones shattered. The unlucky pilot was simply ripped to pieces.

Chiana licked her lips.

Jansz's game was a dangerous one, but at least she understood it. All she had to do was avoid eye contact, obey orders and she'd have every opportunity to make a clean getaway with all the loot she could ever . . .

"Chiana." Jansz sought her, mono-voiced, as deck hands removed the shattered Sciorrcco.

"Yes . . . Lord?"

Satisfied at her response, Jansz glanced at Vurid. The Facilitator was fastidiously grooming his stinger. At Jansz's look he sprang quiveringly to attention.

"One wishes to welcome you aboard, Chiana." Jansz's voice was almost melodic. "There is a ceremony the crew likes to hold. It involves intoxicants, of course, and . . . some . . . other matters. The crew would be very appreciative if you saw fit to join them."

It wasn't an invitation, and Chiana knew it.

"That would be . . . very nice."

"One is sure in one's heart of hearts that you will prove to be a valuable member of the crew . . . particularly with regard to the rescue of the Lady Nyaella Skitrovex and the recovery of our fortunes!"

The crew roared their approval.

What did Jansz mean? Nyaella had no money. She was his prisoner—wasn't she?

Chiana tasted blood on her lips.

"Vurid, call the crew aft."

The crew assembled on the flight deck. Hundreds of beings from a dozen different species, all gathered together with a single common aim.

"Split the barrels and let's quaff the noggin!"

The shout stirred a rousing cheer from the crew.

"Break out the belly-timber!" someone yelled.

A hundred arms and tentacles waved; hands and boots and claws clapped thunder from the sodden air.

Crouched quiveringly upon a small pyramid of sealed barrels, Vurid waited.

"Give us a rind of your special tincture, Vurid!"

The Facilitator arched his back, stinger raised. The crowd fell silent. Hushed expectancy. Jansz stepped onto the deck. He waited, lapping up the hush, stroking the crew with crawling beetle eyes. Then, choir-voiced, he spoke.

"What do you do when you sight a Leviathan?"

And a chorus of voices answered.

"Sing out for her!"

"Good! What next?"

"Away with the boats and after her!"

Jansz moved, slow, rocking as if perched foursquare on a ship of the line. "And what song do you sing as you chase her?" A single voice became a duo, a trio, the harmony rousing.

"Dead Leviathan or a blown drive!"

"Yeeeesssss . . ."

Jansz pulled a plastic box from his tunic. He rubbed it on his tunic until it shone like molten silver. "You see this," he whispered.

Chiana watched the crew. They saw.

"A recent trade and a thing more precious than gold. The Beatles' *White Album*. He who owns this commands a price beyond measure. Wine. Women. Men. A price beyond measure."

To a man, the crew leaned in, wide-eyed.

"Now listen well, for whomsoever among you raises me a brown-backed Leviathan, with wounds in her earthen hide like twisted roots, with betrayal on her tongue and a beating heart of royal Hynerian gold; whomsoever of you raises me this Leviathan he will have this disc!"

"But she's dead, Lord. The Leviathan is dead. The sun took her."

Jansz's voice rose from a whisper to an oratory, layer upon layer of harmonic overtones, a wall of sound that struck through the crew like blue sunlight striking through clouds.

"She is not dead!" he roared. "I feel her golden heart beating in her breast! This is what you've shipped for! This is what I call you to! We'll chase that brownback

through stellar cloud and solar flare until she spouts
black blood and rolls fin-out—and her beating heart of
gold is mine again."

The crew was silent.

Chiana watched them carefully.

"What do you say? Will you marry hands on it? You
look like a valiant bunch."

The crew roared.

"Good! Now let's seal the pact!"

The bear-like skull inclined toward Vurid. The Facilitator produced several casks full of yellow spheres.
The crew gave voice to their approval.

"Fruit. We got fruit!"

"Fermented is best!"

"Save me the pips!"

"Sting 'em Vurid! Give us your special tincture!"

Vurid stung baskets of fruit and tossed them to the
frenzied crew.

Chiana had not taken her eyes off the increasingly intoxicated crew. Hard individuals from the hardest
species. They were rough, they were callous, they
were loyal.

They were stupid.

They were drunk.

Chiana smiled. Fortune smiles on a patient thief.

She moved towards Jansz. He stood apart from the
crew, and took no fruit. Vurid was with him, and both
stood close to the clear wall beyond which they could
see the flaming blue supergiant in the distance.

"She's there, Vurid. Somewhere in those flaming
azure reefs. One knows it. One feels it."

"Despite Lord Jansz's great wisdom, and . . . if Lord

will pardon contradiction . . . Vurid considers this proposition unlikely."

Jansz laughed. "Why the long face, Vurid, old friend? You were present at one's birth; one's earliest memory is of you. Together we have roamed and robbed the Seven Galaxies. Are you no longer game for the chase? Has one's gift for legitimate business robbed your spirit of its fire?"

Vurid quivered. "Vurid is game for death if that is part of business Vurid came for."

Jansz gazed upwards through the transparent canopy, into space. He considered the flaming blue orb that filled a fair third of the sky.

"She vexes one, Vurid. Nyaella vexes one and one shall have her."

Vurid said nothing.

"One knows what she is doing now. She's on that planet. Interfering."

Vurid said nothing. Chiana listened, too, fascinated.

"A Leviathan can carry a good-sized cargo, Vurid. A good-sized cargo. One knows this Hynerienne and she plots. She plots to steal our fair business. And to think that once one sought her hand."

At last, Vurid spoke. "Vurid came here to hunt fortunes, not Lord Jansz's vengeance. How much treasure will vengeance yield, Vurid asks?"

Jansz whirled, the bear-like skull moving smoothly, an ambling avalanche of flesh and sinew masking a mind not to be diverted from its chosen course. "My vengeance will fetch a great premium *here*." Jansz's clenched fist hammered his own chest, the ribs caging his living heart. "And in one's vault, of course." The fist unclenched, fingers like pistons tenderly tracing the Facilitator's ornamented carapace. "Need one remind you that it was your idea to court Nyaella Skitrovex? Must all be fortune with you, Vurid?"

Chiana's eyes narrowed as she observed this interplay. Clearly the relationship between Jansz and Vurid ran far deeper than she had at first supposed. Perhaps if she listened some more she would be able to find something out. Something important, which she could turn to her . . .

"Chiana." The familiar Jansz, now. His voice a purring duet, his eyes locked to hers, crawling. "One observes that you have not taken fruit with the crew. Perhaps . . ." his voice lowered to an intimate solo, ". . . that is wise, all things considered."

Chiana remembered Vurid's stinger, injecting micro-measures of neurotoxin into the fruit.

A stimulant?

A drug?

"Please." Jansz beckoned with one pair of hands. The invitation was clear. Taking Chiana by the hand, Jansz swung back towards the crew. His introspection vanished, swallowed up so fast in the dominant persona he now projected that Chiana was hard pressed to believe she had witnessed that more reflective side to Jansz at all.

"The time has come!" Jansz's voice was the roar of a crowd, and his own crowd responded to it in a way that was becoming predictable to Chiana. "The inauguration will take place now. Bring out the prisoners!"

The next moment Chiana felt something come undone in her heart. Two figures were brought onto the deck. Chains rattled around their bodies. Their heads were covered in black hoods, but their clothes were all too familiar. Chiana involuntarily took a step back. They couldn't know that she had betrayed them. But she knew.

Jansz roared, "See here the evidence that one's golden heart still beats within that devious brown-back. For if these can survive, so, too, can Nyaella Skitrovex."

He pulled off the hoods to reveal Aeryn and Crichton. They saw her and their eyes locked.

"Chiana!" Aeryn's angry shout rang across the deck. "Tell your friends to let us go."

Chiana said nothing.

Her mind swung, like a pendulum, back and forth across time, to all the ugly moments of her life. She saw Halpern Frahn, dying, choking his last breath at her through a clot of his own life's blood.

"Vurid," Jansz said.

As the Facilitator offered Chiana the gun, she knew what she would be asked to do. And she knew that she would do it. Nervelessly, she reached out to take the weapon. It was heavy and cold in her hand.

She wanted to protest, to resist a little, but, finally, she knew she would do what Jansz wanted. After all, she had little choice. She had thrown in her lot with the trader and had nowhere else to go. She had seen how ruthless he could be. She steeled herself and waited for him to say something.

Jansz spoke, a hushed solo. "Each new member of my inner retinue must prove himself or herself worthy. Your task is simple."

Chiana felt her heart lurch. Old memories. "Frak you! I won't kill them."

Still in a whispered solo, Jansz said, "You don't

have to kill them. Just prove yourself. Prove your loyalty. You choose how."

Aeryn and Crichton seemed dumbstruck. Crichton's face was smooth with shock, while anger was just beginning to flare on Aeryn's countenance.

"And if I don't?"

"Nothing. You will leave my service."

Chiana hesitated. All was silent.

"Did you think one would kill you for disobedience?" Jansz asked. "One would not waste such a valuable resource. One does not hold life so cheaply."

Chiana smiled bitterly, remembering the unfortunate Sciorrcco. "I have no money and nowhere to go. Nowhere in space. You know that."

Jansz said nothing.

"So evicting me is the same as killing me, isn't it?"

Jansz said nothing.

Chiana hefted the gun.

She looked at Crichton. Aeryn.

Prove yourself. You choose how.

Her mind whirled. Was this a trick? Some kind of test? If she betrayed her friends, then she had the potential for betraying Jansz. Was that it? Was the test not to shoot?

If it was, how could she tell?

How far was she prepared to go to find out?

What would Jansz do to her if she guessed wrong?

The slight trembling of Chiana's hand betrayed the dreadful turmoil in her mind. She felt Halpern Frahn's eyes boring into hers. Accusing eyes, homing in on her, grasping and holding, even from the past, even in death, refusing to surrender their dreadful grip.

She had to cut loose, had to run, run from the past, from death.

Had to run forward to life, even if death were the key.

Chiana grasped the gun as a drowning man would grasp a life belt.

What if she did not have to kill?

Prove yourself. You choose how.

She lifted the gun. The barrel trembled as her hand shook.

Aeryn and Crichton were staring at her, eyes wide in shock, the questions only just beginning to form, incredulous, disbelieving. Questions to which there would be only one answer. An answer they would never understand, yet one of which they would form an integral part.

A dreadful hush fell.

The crew gazed on.

Chiana turned to the Facilitator. "Sting me a fruit, Vurid. Ten seconds from now I'm going to want to forget this ever happened."

She bit into the offered fruit, felt juice splash across her lips and chin. Her mind splashed, too, back and forth through the bloated moments of her life.

Halpern was Crichton was Aeryn was Halpern was dead was

She raised the gun.

Aimed it at

Halpern

Crichton

An agonized moan unwinding in her throat as she

laughing playfully as she

pulled

the
past-present clicked into perfect focus
trigger
click!
such a small sound and
the gun discharged and
John Crichton, human, astronaut, and reluctant ambassador, stared disbelievingly at the steaming wound in his side, and then toppled slowly, heavily to the deck.

Chiana
aimed
the
gun
at
Aeryn.

Their eyes locked.
Her finger curled on the trigger.
A single tear wrenched itself from her eye as she tightened her grip.

CHAPTER 8

Stars are the engines that drive all life in the universe. They are the source of the raw materials, the essentials.

Heavy elements, which form the basic building blocks of life across myriad species and a billion galaxies, all have one thing in common: they began life in a star. Stars sustain the universe, fuel it with life until their fires die.

But stars are also killers. Their gravity, their radiation—their sheer ferocity—see to that.

The blue supergiant was one of the oldest, the largest, most cantankerous stellar objects that could be viewed by eye or instrument anywhere in the local sky.

By any standards, the blue supergiant was a killer. Swelling up to four hundred times its original size and cooling proportionally, the star had killed all life on every world it had ever captured, absorbing the inner worlds and charring the surfaces of those on which life might normally have flourished.

It waited now only for its inevitable death.

Soon it would go supernova. What would be left of the shattered corpse of its corona would be a lumpen mass of iron, probably no larger than a small moon. The sullen nuclear fire that had burned so tenaciously down the millennia and had spread a ghostly crown of photonic material, across light years, would be no more.

So, eventually, the killer would die and with it would go a large area of local real estate.

Of the local species, those capable of generating their own interstellar technology had been moving out for millennia. Those that could not had been left to their own devices, to buy, trade, beg, or steal a ride to a less dangerous section of the cosmos as best they could before the inevitable catastrophic explosion.

The blue star had been dying for a very long time and there were not many cultures left.

In fact, there was only one.

Its name was Re and it lived on an ocean world orbiting just within the photosphere of the blue supergiant. Beyond the reach of eyes or telescope, Re lived, as it had lived for millennia, in peaceful isolation. Re had been alone in this unnamed world for a long, weary time—longer than the documented histories of many interplanetary cultures.

Re had evolved from a fascinating example of the diversity that the universe had called forth from stellar dust. The species comprised billions of microscopically tiny individuals living in and around the lava tubes that spewed a constant stream of magma from the interior of its world. They sustained life by absorbing heat directly from these lava vents and converting it into energy.

The species was very old, the oldest on the planet, and had developed intelligence millions of years before larger life forms had evolved. Thus it was more than capable of holding its own against savage would-be predators when they appeared.

But the maturing, questing intelligence of the species set questions, and sought to break down boundaries. Individually, they were tiny and their ocean world vast, but that did not inhibit it. A rich and complex culture developed, a restless society facing, even inventing, new challenges all the time. And, occasionally, extraordinary individuals appeared, visionaries capable of changing everything.

Re was such a being.

Re was very special, a little larger than its peers, and blessed with a truly creative imagination. For Re, life began in one of the thousands of gnarled, twisting, gloriously luminescent lava-tube maze-cities that hugged the kilometer-high columns of rock connecting the crust plates to the seabed, and that made the ocean world a labyrinth of pockets of water and weed. Re grew rapidly, its protoplasmic shell tough and flexible, the cilia that produced movement through the water longer and more powerful than any of its generation. And this strong and superior body housed an extraordinary mind, one that questioned everything and thought deeply.

Re tentatively suggested answers to the questions posed by all intelligent life—who am I? How did I get here? What is my role? What is my destiny?—and gave voice to these opinions in public forums. Some, the more conservative, were outraged, but others saw Re as a prophet, even a messiah, and flocked to follow it.

Re and its followers founded a new city, eaten from new lava-tubes, their magma spent and cooled into a twisted fantasmagoria of rock. It became a symbol for life and imagination and it flourished.

Surrounded by like-minded individuals, Re continued to think and postulate, to dream and imagine, to consider the impossible. Inspired, Re proposed a new way for its people to live.

Innovative, radical, revolutionary, and dangerous, the idea was that they lived not as individuals but as a group, a gestalt, with a collective consciousness that would far surpass the many individual minds of which it was composed. Thus a new organism began to take shape and a new consciousness was born. A new Re.

But this new being was perceived as an aberration, a monster, by the rest of the culture, which set aside their fear and acted. Re was hunted down and eventually captured, though to no avail. Any argument put forward to condemn Re was easily countered by the extraordinary intelligence of the gestalt. The gestalt argued eloquently and elegantly, offering the prospect of new sciences, new medical skills, new art, new philosophy, a new perspective on the universe.

The shockwaves split the formerly stable culture into thousands of warring factions and what followed was, for Re, a horror it would never forget. The factions began to fight for the power that would come through the possession of Re. The once-unified civilization waged many bloody, brutal, savage wars. Billions died.

Wracked by guilt, Re fled to the deepest reaches of the ocean world, hiding among the maze of glowing clefts spewing magma. Above it, total war raged, as a species fought itself to exhaustion and eventual extinction. For centuries Re brooded, hoping to forget that the gestalt had been responsible for the suicidal clan warfare of its own species. But the gestalt couldn't forget or forgive itself for what it had caused.

As the millennia passed and the planet's sun swelled, the ocean world heated up and other species perished. Re looked forward to peace at last when the blue supergiant died.

But, as that time approached, Re realized something extraordinary. The gestalt did not want to die. Although an overwhelming guilt consumed its collective mind, the millions of individuals thrived in the rich, volcanic heat. They fed, lived, and bred, producing new generations, all of which were Re. They had a raw lust for life that Re could not ignore. And Re's great mind reached out, beyond their world.

Re was brooding and waiting, reflecting on what it had learned, when it found the possibility of life.

Gazing up, seeing in intimate detail the subtle effects of gravity on tides, looking out through the global ocean, beyond the skin of rock that bounded its world, through the sullen ebb and flow of azure fire that lapped at the vacuum that surrounded the planet, Re saw a comet.

Or was it a spaceship?

Re couldn't be sure. It was small, speed-blurred and indistinct. Approaching very fast. Too fast. And on a collision course.

But, whatever it was, Re recognized hope.

The comet named Moya fell, tearing a hole through space, a whirling blot in the cauldron of the sun, slashing down through layer after layer of super-excited molecules. Her skinsteel hull was peeling away in layers, a fine sloughing of vaporized organotechnology.

Falling, she twisted in space.

Hot! Too hot!

Cradled within the cathedral-chamber, Pilot burned, too.

His mind, bonded to Moya's, saw what she saw, felt what she felt.

Identity lost as, fused, he fell.

Two as one.

A life he would now surrender as she surrendered hers, to the flaming nuclear insanity that flayed her skin and mind.

Elsewhere inside Moya, four additional lives hung in balance. For D'Argo and Zhaan, Rygel and Nyaella, the living ship was close to becoming their tomb. Worse, their cremation fire.

The stink of barbecued starship assaulted their nostrils. Smoke rushed through the chamber with every agonized breath Moya struggled to produce for them.

Slowly the air grew hotter, and the burning stench grew worse as Moya's lungs became choked with poisons her own body was producing, and which she was no longer able to recycle into life-sustaining compounds.

The virus packets in her bloodstream, designed to rebuild vital organs damaged by the necrosis contracted from Crichton, died by the billions. Radiation from the blue star triggered mutant growth that the remnants of her own shattered immune system tried and failed to kill.

Blotched with tumours, skin flayed and mind close to delirium, Moya fell. And with their bodies now so close to death, other minds fell also.

Back through life and love and memory.

A desperate and all too temporary escape.

The Winter Palace—the Palace of Moons—hugged the scalloped ice-volcanoes of the northern continent of Hyneria.

Rygel the New would come here to think, to wonder, sometimes just to find a moment of stillness in a life that was growing ever more full of meaningless social events.

His parents were no longer the sprightly, wrinkled creatures he remembered from his childhood. They were growing old, smooth. It was common knowledge that the abdication might happen any time now. The exact date was not known, of course, but Rygel found himself becoming more and more apprehensive of that inevitable day the more tightly he became bound in the pomp and circumstance surrounding the preparations for his own coronation.

If his parents were old, what of Rygel himself? Now in his fortieth cycle, Rygel the New had grown into a

mature, calm individual, whose loyalty to his father
and crown was paramount. The fact that he did not like
any aspect of his royal life beyond the occasional and
treasured conversations with old Noonspurner, snatched
at private moments during the night, was their secret.
His wishes were of no consequence. His father had set
young Rygel a single, simple rule to live by, and Rygel
the New had subsequently lived a life to make his father proud.

*A Dominar must never be eclipsed by his own
shadow.* That had been the rule, the yardstick by
which he had measured his slowly maturing life. He
had observed it well. He was engaged now to a Hynerienne named Inandulla. Hailing from a distant branch
of the Hynerian royal family, Inandulla was both
beautiful and intelligent—not at all boring, really. She
had been adjudged by the Powers That Be as the perfect vessel with which he could shape the future of the
Hynerian royal bloodline.

Inandulla seemed perfectly happy to accept the proposed marriage to Rygel. As a youth he had been a re-
markable specimen and his wealth, beauty, and wit
had simply matured with age. That he was also no
sluggard in the pre-nuptial (and highly illicit) marriage
pond experiments they had secretly carried out, went
entirely without saying, of course. But it was an important factor.

The royal viziers had done their jobs well. Rygel
and Inandulla were little short of a perfect match.

And yet . . .

Something in Rygel yearned for the one thing his
perfectly appropriate and cleverly assigned beloved
was absolutely unable to provide . . . spontaneity. Happy

accidents. The thrill of never knowing quite what was going to happen next.

Serendipity.

Plain and simple.

He got what he wanted sooner than expected.

When the first secret note from Nyaella, pleading for a clandestine meeting, arrived anonymously beneath the door of his chambers at the Palace of Moons, Rygel knew immediately that serendipity was something he should never have wished for. He burned the letter as soon as he'd read it, scattered the ashes to the snowy wastes from the stone lintel where once he had sat with its author, long into the night, star-gazing and speaking in excited tones of their future together.

Rygel felt his heart burn with the letter, felt it burst under the grip of cold decision, scatter joy and love and hope to the barren snows with the cold ash.

Twisting, hull peeling, she fell. The comet-Moya drew a shining path into the star, a gold-tipped arrow shining through azure fire. Down from the edge of space she came, tumbling and dying, molten skin a golden veil that seeped into the blue fire, control gone, mind bursting with a fire all its own, the death fire of electrical impulses run wild in a brain unable to recognize its own impending dissolution . . .

For Delvians, the ultimate Seek was for spiritual Unity. Rarely, if ever, did such unity take place, and when it did the circumstances surrounding the occasion had to be something incredible.

Zhaan herself had achieved spiritual Unity only once before, despite her relatively great age and experience. There were reasons why, of course. Reasons that remained, despite the depth-healing and spiritual realignment rituals.

Love. That was a good enough reason.

Hate was another.

Mostly, though, for Zhaan anyway, it was fear.

Fear of the thing that her priesthood drove her towards with an overwhelming force she could never deny.

Because the only time she had ever achieved true spiritual unity with another the result had been cold-blooded murder.

She had slain the man she loved. Murdered him in cold blood at the moment of deepest intimacy. The man who in his waking mind and his sleep had held her image as dear as his own beating heart.

Her actions had sundered her order, creating a rift of shattering incomprehension. She was Pa'u Zotoh Zhaan, and had reached the Tenth Level in the Delvian Seek. As close to enlightenment as anyone her age had ever been. Bitaal and she were betrothed.

Why had she killed him? For Zhaan, the reason had been overwhelmingly simple: Bitaal had planned to betray their order, their culture, their entire world.

Betray everything that his spiritual teaching had ever been a symbol for.

Belief shattered, Zhaan had fled.

Fled her order, her life, her world.

But they had caught her and imprisoned her. She had escaped, but she could not escape her guilt.

Somewhere in the universe there was a way she could heal herself. Somewhere there was a ritual, a spiritual grail she could seek that could enable her to achieve understanding . . . that and redemption. Until then she would run.

But over the cycles, Zhaan was to learn a dreadful truth. No matter how far and how fast she ran, she could never escape the last moment of Bitaal's life. The last moment of their life together.

The touch of his last breath on her lips, warm from his touch.

The last azure flush of life's blood in his cooling cheeks.

The question upon his lips.

Why?

Why did you do this?

But he knew.

Down through the coronal crown the comet-Moya fell . . . down through the flaming photosphere . . . deeper into the flaming skin of the supergiant . . . until, incredibly, the shock of the impossible impinged upon her mind . . . and some last measure of sanity awoke.

Flight or fight.

She was in shadow.

The planet sped towards the comet-Moya. Her mind shut down, finally, unable to calculate an approach vector. Consciousness fled. She hurtled down, caught in the wake of two gigantic gravity pools.

Collision course.

The planet was soft. The impact shallow. Conflicting gravitational gradients had seen to that. Luck, of a kind.

Moya struck, flaming.

Bounced.

Struck again.

Smashed into a mountainous shelf of rock.

Tumbled through the crust into shocking liquid cold.

Pilot opened his eyes—and felt surprise as they filled instantly with water. Water that pressed against his body, against the limbs and connections, the vaulted cathedral chambers of his nerve conduits and muscle pistons.

For a time measurable only to one with senses as finely honed as his own, Pilot wanted only to scream. Panic. Fear. Where was the air? Where was the scent of his symbiotic partner?

Pilot successfully repressed a confused spectrum of emotions, processing chemical suppressants and injecting them into his body to control his autonomic reactions.

His heart valves slowed from their panicky fibrillation . . . slowed . . .

. . . slowed . . .

. . . finally assuming the pulsar-regular beat of normal life.

He inhaled. Deep breath.

Calm. Still.

There was air here. The water was richly oxygenated. He would not drown.

And the scent of Moya was still pervasive, saturating every molecule that strained through his chambered lungs.

Moya was *alive.*

Unfortunately, Pilot's joy was short lived. He could now detect an odd set of hormonal triggers in the water around him.

Alien signatures.

Coming closer.

His apprehension increased. A feeling from a source as strange to him as anything he had yet experienced, with an effect that was as terrifying as it was confusing. Memories that were not his own flooded through his mind, an overwhelming tide, dragging him through another's conception, birth, growth.

In a space of time that in all probability could never have been measured, Pilot felt all that it meant to be another. An entire second life smashed into a space of time defined by one beat of his own madly racing heart. His body spasmed, neurochemical fire breaching one synaptic firebreak after another, running before the wind of shock at a speed faster than thought itself. His mind, a unique and highly articulate biological construction, lost instantly its ability to process any kind of higher thought in the first touch of this experiential set.

Cognitive ability lost, unable to reason, Pilot regressed to an inarticulate animalistic state. Coma was the inevitable result.

Coma—and memories.

Memories of another.

Memories of . . .

Of . . .

Pilot slept and, with Moya, was absorbed by the living colloidal soup that knew itself as Re.

Re carefully studied this comet . . . and discovered that it wasn't a comet at all. It wasn't a thing, but a life form. The first Re had encountered in more time than it cared to consider.

It was a Leviathan. That was what it called itself. Moya.

And it was dying.

Re recognized necrosis and radiation damage—acres of burns. But Re also realized that the life form could perhaps be a bargaining counter, something with which the gestalt could trade.

Re pondered briefly and acted swiftly. It was obvious to Re that a dead life form had no value to the godlike being who had offered it passage away from its doomed solar system, and who had agreed to stand by in the event that Re would be able to think of a suitable barter. The Leviathan would have to be healed.

Re studied the problem from within and without, allowing particles of itself to enter and soothe, to study and comprehend. The Leviathan felt fear and pain. Its hull and peripherals were damaged. It was blind. These were all simple physiological processes, easily alleviated, easily mended. But there was also necrotic virus coursing through Moya's body. This was a much more complex problem, even for a mind such as Re's.

Re entered into symbiosis with Moya, absorbing blood, filtering and cleansing, allowing the now infected parts of its own gestalt to drift away on the ocean currents, to die. The sacrifice was worthwhile. Re felt responsible for so much death that it eagerly seized upon the opportunity to preserve life.

With the blood that Re absorbed came chemicals; and the proteins and hormones of many different species. And Re recognized memories. And not only memories. There were other life forms present too.

Re considered.

Perhaps the creatures living inside Moya were subsets of the Leviathan's memories. But they could be physical elements of Moya with limited autonomy. They could even be individuals in their own right. It was a puzzle, but it was unimportant. All that mattered to Re was that these beings were alive, and that Re had an opportunity to heal.

Re again slipped into the Leviathan, warming, mending, calming. It wrapped itself around all the life forms it found inside, enveloping them in a soothing sleep.

CHAPTER 9

Rygel, Nyaella, Zhaan, D'Argo, Pilot, and Moya, warmed and comforted by Re, slept deeply. And remembered.

It was his fifteenth year as Dominar and the fifth since his father and mother had died. The teaweed lay fallow after heavy solar rain and the gypsy wine-treaders balked in their thousands from work that earned them little reward beyond a good raga and free mother's ruin. It was in his fifteenth year as Dominar that the unthinkable happened. Destiny came to the Palace of Moons.

She came during the time of solitude, when three moons met in the inky night above the ice-capped mountain ramparts.

Rygel gently folded the papyrus back into its leather case and touched the seal. The case filled a particular space in a single bookshelf in the most private reading room of the great palace library.

Reflecting the palace itself, and the three moons for which it was named, the library consisted of three circular chambers, their vaulted roofs stained-glass domes. Arched buttresses erupted from the thousands of shelves lining the masonry walls, stone bones amidst a flesh of leather spines. Glowjars hung from intricately worked brackets, the flickering pond-life within providing ample, if subdued, lighting. A safer alternative to candles and, Rygel felt, a more attractive one.

The papyrus he had been studying was ancient, passed down through family generations since the time of Rygel X. Hundreds of cycles. Held in this slim volume was a simple wisdom. One his father had never let him forget: *a Dominar must never be eclipsed by his own shadow.*

The all-too real reminder of the practical upshot of this piece of family wisdom now cast her own shadow across the great walls of books over which the three moons hung so gloriously.

"Nyaella. How did you get past the guards?"

"I had to see you. Do you know why?"

"I can guess. You should not be here. It will be dangerous for us both if you are caught."

She came further into the light. "That's what I love about you. You always say exactly what you mean."

"People change."

"You haven't changed. You might think you have, but you haven't."

"What do you want me to say?"

"That she's wrong for you."

"She's wrong for me."

"That you'll make me your queen."

"I can't. You know that."

She came closer. Her perfectly seamed brow wrinkled, her eyes holding his, her scent overpowering. "Say you love me."

Rygel stood suddenly. The ancient bamboo reading table flipped over. A blotter and several quills fell to the marbled floor.

"If I say that, then everything changes."

"Yes."

She moved closer. "Say it, Rygel. Say you love me. Or say it isn't true, and I'll leave. You'll never see me again."

"I . . ."

She waited.

"I . . . *I don't love you.*"

She backed away, eyes wide with disbelief and hurt. "I don't believe you."

"You have to go now."

She turned, hesitated, turned back abruptly. "The Queen loves your cousin Bishan. They are planning to depose you. Noonspurner knows."

Nyaella ran from the library.

Rygel tried not to hear her sobs.

He did not see her again for more than three hundred cycles. By then the Queen was dead, old Noonspurner was dead and Rygel himself had lost an empire.

Aeryn had been placed in a drab cell aboard Jansz's ship. There was no furniture. No viewscreens. No handle on the inside of the door.

Aeryn had been left here to make a decision.

Why had Chiana done it? Why had she turned on them? Her own crewmates? They who had taken her in and given her shelter, protection. Had she been forced to do it? Perhaps there were circumstances they were unaware of.

Certainly a shot from a weapon such as the one Chiana had used should have been fatal. Yet Crichton—though badly wounded—still lived.

Why?

Aeryn sighed. Trying to understand the motivations of someone like Chiana was pointless. Though Chiana had only been aboard Moya for a short time, she had instantly shown herself to be among the most self-centered beings Aeryn had ever met. Chiana was very much a question mark. No one aboard Moya really knew or trusted her.

And so the question remained—why shoot?

Could she have thought an attack on her former crewmates would endear her to Jansz in some way, for some reason of her own?

Was Chiana really that stupid?

There was of course, no answer. Aeryn sat in her cell, hugging her knees, thinking about Crichton. Thinking back to the moment when, standing beside the wounded astronaut and trying to prepare herself for a similar lethal gunblast, Aeryn had instead been offered a trade. Her knowledge of weapons in exchange for Crichton's life. Jansz seemed very interested in acquiring her as he had Chiana, for his crew.

She had agreed, of course. It had been expedient: Crichton had been taken to the ship's apothecary and his life saved. And now she had a decision to make.

Should she make good on the deal? Granted, it had been a deal made under duress and therefore was not morally binding. But Crichton remained within Jansz's power. And Aeryn was trapped—to quote a phrase of John's—between a rock and a hard place.

At this moment the door opened and Chiana entered unannounced. Aeryn did not bother getting to her feet. She simply stared. Chiana returned the stare with the hint of a frown. *Was that disapproval?* Aeryn laughed contemptuously.

"Aeryn, they'll take you in," Chiana began. "You'll have to earn your place here like everyone else, but it's worth it. It's a chance to belong to something again."

Chiana's voice was soft, almost persuasive.

But all Aeryn could think about was the wound Chiana had made in Crichton's belly, the look on his face as he fell, and his moans as he was carried to the apothecary. Chiana was chilled to the bone by Aeryn's expression.

Knees hugged to her chest, Aeryn replied, "Don't try to sweet-talk me, Chiana. I played your game. I traded my strong gun-arm with Jansz for Crichton's life. I'm a woman of my word. But don't expect me to be grateful." Aeryn took a breath, felt the anger coiling deep inside like a serpent. "You know, we're all part of Jansz's little head game; you, me, all of us. John was right—he's amusing himself with us. Now, I know that's a thing you seem to enjoy. But not me. So just keep your justifications and your platitudes and your phony concern to yourself."

"Whatever." Chiana shrugged offhandedly, seemingly unaffected by Aeryn's response. "It's your life."

Aeryn snorted with disgust. "Just tell me what they

want me to do. If it's sign an oath in blood, fine. If it's shoot a friend, you can tell them to shove it right up alongside your justifications, platitudes, and sympathy."

For a moment, Chiana's perfectly composed face clouded.

Aeryn studied the little traitor closely. Was that a crack in her highly polished veneer? Chiana rubbed her eyes with the back of her fist. Aeryn was suddenly struck by how childlike the gesture was. How childlike the woman was, for that matter.

"You don't get it, do you?" Chiana said with a humorless laugh. "You PK drones never get it. I'm handing you a chance at life . . ."

". . . by getting high on illegal fruit and *shooting my friend!*"

". . . and you're tossing it right *down the recycle chute!*"

"Now you just . . ."

"No, Officer Aeryn-high-and-mighty-Sun, you 'just'! You just frelling listen to me for once. You might even find it interesting."

"I doubt it."

Ignoring Aeryn's sarcasm, Chiana continued. "You don't know anything about feelings—or else why would you have ever been a Peacekeeper? Moya is dying, probably dead. And it's all Crichton's fault. Why shouldn't he pay for it? What did he ever do for us? He's just a stupid alien. Just a stupid alien with a death wish who, despite being coddled every waking moment by people who should know better, got all of us in this fix with his stupid toothache! And which," she added breathlessly, "as you already said, is something that even a *child* would not be stupid enough to do!"

Chiana drew another breath and then continued, even more viciously. "Not that I wanted to live on that frelling ship, with its stupid crew. No, what do I care for a bunch of self-righteous moralizers who wouldn't recognize a lucky break if it blacked their eye with a gold bar, or understand what it was like to make a life-or-death decision every day since you could first tell the difference? To know how it felt to have nothing, no food in your belly, no credit in your account, no love in your heart for anything—or anyone."

Aeryn suddenly became aware that somewhere along the line Chiana's questions had stopped being questions and were attempts to explain her actions. A strange sensation came over Aeryn, and her expression softened slightly.

"And don't even *think* about feeling sorry for me. In this life there are two sorts of people, Aeryn. Survivors and corpses. We both know which I am. Which are you?"

Aeryn said nothing.

"I guess we'll be finding out soon," Chiana added. "Jansz wants you tested in combat."

"Against you, I hope."

"Sorry to disappoint you—against Vurid. He's a killer. Be on your toes."

And with that, Chiana walked away.

Aeryn watched her leave. She had wanted to smash her fists into that porcelain-smooth face.

But she couldn't think of a single thing to say.

Re cocooned Moya and everything in her in sweet, re-freshing and healing sleep. The gestalt listened to the tumult of memories, learned to distinguish among the individual beings and learned compassion.

Rygel's childhood upbringing, his arrogance, his thwarted ambition and the memories of his love both fascinated and moved Re.

The raw emotional wounds of D'Argo as he relived the discovery of the body of his murdered wife over and over again disturbed Re. Moreover, it forced Re to realize that it could heal and relax bodies but not minds; there were limits to its powers.

But most of all, it monitored Moya, felt her recover, grow stronger with every passing arn. Her grip on life, at first so tenuous, grew more tenacious, and Re knew that it would soon be time to contact the godlike being again.

Chiana ran. Through the metal-walled passages of Jansz's ship, past stalls and tents, through the crowded marketplace. She ignored the cries and leers, gave no thought to the stares or gestures she generated, the lecherous glances of sundry male life forms.

She had to run.

Away from Aeryn Sun.

Away from John Crichton.

Away from Halpern Frahn.

Away from the terrible things she had done.

Huddled in the hydroponics garden, shivering beneath a broad-leafed fern, Chiana squeezed her eyes shut to block out the leaves, the UV lamps, the ribbed dome, the rabid flare of the blue supergiant and immeasurably further away, the billion distant, heartless points of light that were the stars.

Chiana bit back the tears that threatened to fill her eyes. She dug her fingers into the soft loam. Wondered briefly how much a stolen bucketful would fetch on the open market. Rubbing the black soil between her fingers, Chiana could not stop the tears. The soil was rich with life. Gravid with minerals and chemicals, potential from which new life must spring. Even this dirt—even this was so much richer than her life had ever been.

Until Halpern Frahn, of course.

Then—for a brief few cycles at least—she had known what true happiness could mean. How it could shape a life, a heart.

Chiana ground the dirt between her fingers, let it fall back to the ground. Her tears were gone. She would shed no more for herself—and Halpern was dead and so needed none.

If only she hadn't been so naive. Imagining he felt anything at all for her—beyond simple curiosity. She had slept with him, of course she had, a sucker for the attention he paid her, the patience he showed her. He was a respectable man. A businessman. And perhaps it was his wealth as much as anything that had turned her eyes from the truth. That all he wanted was to use her; to barter her for business favors. To him she was little more than a commodity.

By the time she realized this, though, it was too late. She had wanted to believe only the best of him. She had wanted that so much. And for a time it had been that way. Now she knew she had been lying to herself. Well, never again.

That he lied to her was bad enough, that he caused her pain and allowed others to do so as well was worse. But what cut far deeper than this was the knowledge of how much of herself she had surrendered to him. Her life had been so hard, had hurt for so long, had seen so little reward, that surrender was almost inevitable. She wanted to fall. Wanted him to catch her. Wanted to lose the control she had always sought to keep for herself.

Perhaps he had seen that in her, perhaps some kernel of darkness deep inside him had responded in kind. Maybe no one was to blame. Maybe lust and personal ambition weren't at the root of it at all. Maybe it was just people. How bad they could be. A mathematical equation. Input X and Y, and Z is the result.

And was that all she was? An inevitable result of the human equation? Chiana could no more find an answer now than then. All she knew was that eventually he had taken her too far, and she had input a factor into their personal equation that he had not bargained for.

Now he was dead.

And she was free.

Chiana wiped the tears from her cheeks, leaving a child's muddy streaks in their place.

And now she was free? Why did the words sound so much more like a question than a statement?

Chiana huddled beneath the fern as above her a clock ticked, a switch tripped and a fog of warm water vapor blew through the undergrowth, lifting a sweet scent from the ground and leaves. Chiana felt the moisture gather in her hair and on her skin, each drop mirroring the words in her mind; echoing now as they had when she had stood so recently in the apothecary, staring down at Crichton, his body hooked up to dozens of flexible glass tubes—a maze of bell jars and flasks, each filled with bubbling solutions that were being injected into his body in controlled doses. More glass had linked to a tank containing a strange, snail-like organism. The creature was alive. Chiana presumed a process of chemical exchange was taking place between the animal and Crichton.

One life for another.

Why was she so disturbed?

She had no answers. She could only run—run from feelings she did not want and could not endure. But huddled now beneath the damp fern she at least realized why.

Because she was stupid.

Because she had failed Jansz's test.

Prove yourself. You choose how. Those had been his words. She had assumed they meant something they did not. Read into them more than was there. Her life experiences had compelled her to see things in those words that were only present in her head, her memory.

She had thought Jansz wanted her to prove herself to him. In fact, he had only wanted her to show *herself* what she was like.

Was that his sick game? To force a confused and self-deluded young woman to confront her own true nature? To strip away the lies that cloaked her life? To let her understand a little more about herself than she had before?

That had to be it. It had been her choice to fire. Not Jansz's. He had not forced her. The choice had been hers. But why had Jansz done this? The answer, she now realized, was simple. Jansz was a trader. He had made the ultimate trade.

Still huddled beneath the damp fern Chiana finally

understood the choice he had helped her make: she had traded a long, cold, truthful look at herself—a chance to stop lying to herself—against the promise to place herself in Jansz's service.

Chiana couldn't stop the tears. The price she'd paid for knowing herself was the possibility that Crichton would die—and only now did she realize she shouldn't have fired that gun.

The arena was little more than a metal pit scalloped out of the hull and lined with rough-edged deck gratings. A noisy crowd surrounded the pit, yelling and jeering and throwing bits of junk. Aeryn wondered how many of them were currently Jansz's eyes and ears.

She moved into the pit. The walls towered steeply above her, bowing outwards and then in to form a clear dome, through which poured the bleached azure rays of the blue supergiant. More decking hugged the walls, strapped in place with wire. Aeryn ran her hand along the surface, felt old oxide and older stains cling to her fingertips.

She rubbed her fingers together, a tiny circular motion, fingertips grating across the oily granules that clung to the skin.

Would she die here?

Would she die today?

Aeryn promised herself that if she did fall here today then her spirit would come back to haunt this place until everyone in it was dust.

The voice of the crowd surged, crashing over her like surf across jagged rocks. Clear across the pit a grating similar to the one through which she'd entered was pulled roughly open.

Vurid Skanslav scuttled into the pit.

The grating was slammed and tied behind him, wired shut to prevent accidental damage or deliberate escape.

Aeryn took a deep breath.

The Facilitator seemed larger than when she'd first seen him. The blue light from the supergiant bleached out his chitinous body to a grainy silhouette. White edges scored his angular form, the ridges of elastic muscle on arms, the vicious points of legs and stinger.

His clubbed leg hung clear of the ground—it swayed, gently, deceptively gently, a point of focus for an opponent, like a hypnotist's watch. Something to deflect attention when the attack came.

Aeryn was not fooled.

She waited, still, arms at her sides, fingers itching for the trigger of her pulse rifle, a knife, a club, *anything* she could use as a weapon.

Today's wants are tomorrow's obituaries.

That's what her combat instructor had told her. He'd knocked her down after she'd gotten up grinning from a fall, and she never smiled in combat again.

He never knocked her down again, either.

The crowd began to get restless. They were waiting for someone to move, for someone to draw first blood.

Aeryn's heart was pounding, driving her to move, to attack, to do something, anything—but she did nothing. She merely waited. Time could be your ally or your enemy. She was not fighting the crowd.

Not yet, anyway.

So it was Vurid who moved first, a slow sideways crab around the pit. Aeryn moved with him, keeping plenty of room between them, her attention divided between his hands, the vicious points of his legs and that singularly dangerous stinger . . .

"Vur-*rid!*"

"Vur-*rid!*"

"Vur-*rid!*"

The crowd gave voice to its feeling. Aeryn wondered how much of that feeling was Jansz's.

And then the Facilitator moved, really moved, leaping at her with incredible speed, and reaching to grab with all four hands. Aeryn felt the wind of his passing brush her shoulder as she ducked, rolled, and spun away.

She heard something whistle past her ear. A metallic *twangthunk* that terminated in a dented grating, a sludgy clot of dripping venom and a single splashed droplet of clear fluid blotting her cheek.

She wiped it away on her sleeve with her sweat.

"That's it! Give her the old Vurid Special!"

Boy, the crowd really . . . it really . . . Aeryn felt dazed. She swayed, shook off the second of dizziness.

Vurid was coming at her again, low to the ground, legs compressing, preparing to jump. Aeryn crouched, heels pivoting in the grating, no time to breathe as he came up at her, hands clutching, long neck arrow straight.

Aeryn grabbed the nearest limb—a leg—as Vurid leaped at her. He fell backwards and rolled. The chitin point of the limb jammed into the deck grating. A terrible scream. The limb snapped.

Suddenly the world was a blurred twist of motion . . .

But now . . .

Nothing would focus . . .

She had . . .

The light slashed at her eyes . . .

A weapon . . .

A tremendous weight bore her to the deck. Her head banged against the grating and she saw stars. Big *blue* stars. Big *flaming* blue . . .

Then she was moving again, rolling as the weight thudded into her, hands reaching to catch and hold, the muscular neck weaving to smash against her chest and ribs, batter her again and again, as she tried for balance, felt the deck shift under her—*loose grating, damn!*—and she went down again, this time with Vurid on top, and it was as much as she could do to get her hands up to protect herself. Then she felt a jolt as the chitin dagger connected and . . .

. . . *a whipcrack of sound and* . . .

. . . a jolt of fire slashed through her face, the side of her neck, and she jerked upright, shrieked as the pain snapped her head up, eyes wide, pupils black tunnels gathering the bleached blue light and then she was tottering backwards, jerked to one side as the stinger was wrenched from her shoulder and she was falling and Vurid leapt and her hands came up and his full weight landed on her and smashed her back and she lay panting on the deck as a speed-blurred shadow blotted out the bleached light and then

  quite suddenly

  everything

  stopped.

Time seemed to stand still.

Aeryn found herself standing.

Somehow. She didn't know how.

Standing beside the body of Vurid, which was quivering, panting beside her on the deck. The chitin rapier of his own broken foreleg had jammed through the base of his neck and blood was oozing out . . .

The sunlight was very hot and everything looked kind of grainy and washed out. Her head was on fire. Her mind in a blur.

A voice spoke . . .

"Enough! Clear the Pit! Combat has ended!"

But Aeryn Sun did not hear the voice, had no thought of her own life. Instead she heard John Crichton's awful scream. She heard Chiana's pitiful words.

It was as if a giant, raging fireball of a star had exploded in her head, and that star was the life of those she held most dear.

She jerked herself upright, back straightening, head up, eyes fixed on Vurid.

There was a strange noise. A shriek of some kind. It came from her throat.

Suddenly, Aeryn pulled the chitin rapier from Vurid's neck, and plunged it into his heart.

Aeryn looked up. Faces swam into focus. They gazed down at her. Cold. Accusing. When they spoke the voices rolled in sickening waves around and through her head.

"What are you playing at?"

"Are you trying to get us all killed?"

"You will be punished."

Nothing like hospital sympathy.

She tried to move—her arms and legs would not work.

That'll be the neurotoxin, then . . .

Aeryn felt a needle jabbed into her arm. Cold fire

flooded her body. Her heart raced. Her face flushed. Her ears rang.

The apothecary snapped into perfect focus.

Chiana. Jansz.

A bunch of scurrying white-suits.

"I'm alive then?"

Did she really sound that stupid?

"Yes." Jansz. A furious solo. "You are alive. For now."

Jansz's bearlike head loomed closer. His mouths gaped and the sullen tang of sulphuric acid assailed her nostrils.

"Denticed lately?"

The joke rang on deaf ears—but Aeryn felt a bubble of laughter burst in her belly.

"She's hysterical." Chiana's mouth twisted in disgust. "Somebody give her something."

Another jab in her arm and the laughter ended.

Aeryn couldn't turn her head. "Come to dispense the punishment then? What are you going to do, toss me out of an airlock?"

Chiana's face hardened even further. "Why did you kill him?"

"What did you expect me to do, Chiana, stand there meekly and let myself be stabbed and poisoned to death?"

Chiana's lip curled and she moved away. Another bed. A second figure. Crichton. *Great. Now we're both on sick leave.*

Jansz transfixed her with great black orbs. "The fight was not to the death."

"In that case, allow me to compliment you on your absolutely world-class communication skills."

Aeryn felt herself pressed back onto the cot. Jansz's hand easily fitted neatly around her throat. Aeryn's two fists could barely span his armoured fingers. They remained that way for a second.

Aeryn had never felt so helpless.

Chiana turned back, placed a small white hand on Jansz's. It barely covered one of his thumbs. Nevertheless, he removed his hand from Aeryn's throat. "A few days ago I remember you shouting at Crichton for not understanding the rules. How does it feel?"

Aeryn licked dry lips.

"I knew the rules."

Jansz's eyes blazed. Anger. Fear.

Sorrow?

Had she missed something here?

"You can only push me so far, Chiana. You should know that by now. After that the PK training and my own sweet nature kick in and—hey!—I guess we all know what happens then."

Jansz turned away. His hand closed around a nearby equipment stand. The metal folded like wet paper.

Chiana leaned closer. "Vurid was supposed beat you quickly, sting you a little, leave you thinking you were going to die. Then Jansz would have administered the antitoxin and saved your life. You'd have been properly grateful. An amusement for the crowd and a quick lesson in ship's discipline for you."

Aeryn shrugged. "Guess school's out for a while."

"Not really." Jansz turned slowly, eyes crawling.

Aeryn felt a cold fist grip her heart.

Then Jansz would have administered the antitoxin . . .

Jansz nodded slowly, no hint of satisfaction in his duet. "No punishment will be administered. Vurid lived by the same code as all. Aeryn Sun you may have the freedom of the ship—for as long as you have to live."

And he turned abruptly and left the apothecary.

Chiana watched him go and then turned back to Aeryn.

"Survivor or corpse. I guess now we know, don't we?"

And she followed Jansz from the room.

CHAPTER 10

Re concentrated and its collective mind moved out beyond its world, seeking its own salvation. The Leviathan was nearly well enough to awake. It was time to begin bargaining in earnest.

There were things about those onboard that puzzled Re, though it strove to ignore such issues. The strange, conflicting emotions that wracked the priest Zhaan when she thought of her dead lover, for instance. Something like a shudder passed through Re whenever it saw the horrifying image of Zhaan killing him. Re knew that the act was inevitable, even necessary, but it no longer understood murder, and so understanding was not possible.

And the being known as Nyaella Skitrovex was even more of an enigma. The memories that coincided with those of Rygel evoked sympathy and compassion, but more recent memories were darker and perplexing.

Re chose not to worry about them unduly. Instead, it

concentrated on the matter in hand. And made contact. But the voice was different, the mind harder and more subtle, more complex.

"Vurid is no longer with one. But one was waiting for your call," the godlike voice said. "Do you wish to trade with one?"

Where is Vurid? Re asked.

"Vurid is dead."

So much death, Re observed.

"Yes. One will miss him." A pause. "Do you wish to trade?"

I have a trade.

"What do you have?"

A Leviathan.

Vurid should have been buried in space, but Jansz had a different use for his body. As Chiana watched, an honor guard comprising the principal members of Jansz's Compound carried the Facilitator's body to the hydroponics garden. Here it was laid upon a ceramic bier of fruit and vines beneath the cold, unfeeling stars. A single glass tap was set into the side of the bier.

Jansz took his place beside the bier.

"In death we are enriched."

Taking a crystal bottle, Jansz scattered the contents across fruit and corpse.

"Tears for you, my friend."

The smell of fermentation filled the garden. Chiana blinked tears. In moments the body and fruit had melted into slush.

"And a last case of Vurid's special brew for all of us!"

Taking a gold cup, Jansz held it beside the bier and

gave the tap a sharp twist. Liquid trickled into the cup. He lifted the cup and drank, then passed it to the crew. With a rousing cheer, the crew queued for the tap.

Much later, Chiana found herself perched in a small fruit tree, gazing out into space. The blue supergiant blazed nearby. Chiana felt the tree tip slightly as Jansz leaned casually against it, his head level with her own, perched as she was in the lowermost branches.

"Death," she said without looking at Jansz, "is really, really stupid."

Jansz nodded. The bone plates cresting his skull neatly sliced a small branch from the tree. "There are days," he said, one careful voice at a time, "when one feels very strongly that life is really, really stupid also."

Chiana nodded. "I know what you—oops!"

Jansz's hand fitted neatly around her waist, preventing her from toppling from her perch.

"Oh. Thanks." Chiana turned her head carefully. Beside her Jansz gazed out into space. Chiana bit her lip. "I made a mistake once."

"A humanoid?"

"Yes."

Jansz nodded sagely.

"I think I may be making another mistake right now."

Jansz turned slowly to face Chiana.

"One has no wish to sound obvious, though one suspects one is probably too intoxicated to either notice or care. So." Jansz thought for a moment. "At the risk of sounding obvious—which one apologizes for—everybody one ever knew has made a mistake at some time in their life. One has made several oneself. Vurid made—well, only one that ever mattered." Jansz closed his eyes, plated lids closing off those crawling orbs. "Most of the time one is lucky enough to get second chances."

"Peacekeepers don't believe in second chances."

"So one has now learned."

Chiana rubbed the back of her hand across her face. "There's never enough time, is there?"

Jansz sat heavily on the ground beside the fruit tree.

"Tell me about him. About Vurid."

The massive skull inclined slowly. "He was one of one's fathers."

"One of your fathers?"

Jansz sighed. "Our species are symbiotic. The practice is complex . . . and dangerous. But not as rare as you might imagine."

Chiana urged Jansz to continue.

"He was the most intelligent—no. The cleverest—no. One is afraid one does not possess the words."

Chiana placed a comforting hand on the topmost plate of Jansz's skull-crest. She felt the calciferous material flush with blood.

A moment passed.

"The only mistake Vurid ever made," said Jansz in a quiet solo, "was advising one to trade with Nyaella Skitrovex."

Aeryn had often wondered what it would feel like to die. Now she knew. Full of regret.

She lay on the apothecary's cot, trying to get comfortable. No chance. Then again, maybe she did not deserve to get comfortable. She had made an error, a bad one. It had cost her her life. All she had to do now was lie quietly here until she was called on to pay the price. But Aeryn had never been one to lie quietly—under any circumstances.

Turning her head produced only mild pain in her neck now. Simple whiplash after all. She would have laughed but she didn't want to disturb Crichton, whom she knew lay on the cot next to hers.

He was sleeping. Perhaps drugged. Ropes of colored glass tubes ran to and from his body. They passed through a maze of retorts and flasks, in the midst of which was a simple white box. On top of the box was a tank, like one in which she had once kept jellyfish. In the tank was a curious creature. A pink-shelled gastropod, lathered in what looked like worms, suspended in a glass cradle. It moved weakly every now and then, jerking as pistons fed fluid to it or sucked fluid from it.

Crichton twitched whenever the creature did.

Aeryn gathered her thoughts. This must be another of Jansz's miracle cures.

Crichton's eyes were open. He was looking at her.

Aeryn glanced around and then sat up.

No one working in the room took the slightest notice.

She got warily to her feet, pleased to find that she didn't feel too dizzy. She walked to Crichton's cot. His eyes tracked hers. *All the way, baby.*

She reached out for his hand; hesitated; pulled her hand back. She sat beside him, separated by a single sheet of cloth light years wide.

His voice was little more than a croak. "It's bad, isn't it."

"I can't lie to you."

He nodded. "Thought . . . so."

"They had to amputate."

"Oh, God. My legs?"

"Your brain."

"Very funny."

"That's the good news. The bad news is that they saved your sense of humor."

Her smile faded.

And that I'll never see you again.

"That's it in the jar over there." She glanced at the pink creature in the tank. Its movements seemed more agitated now. And there was something familiar about them, almost as if—

"Aeryn, did I ever tell you it hurts when I laugh?"

"Not lately."

"Remind me."

"I'll do that."

"Listen, I . . ." Her voice choked. "There's something I have to do. I have to . . ." His eyes held hers. Did he know what had happened to her? Did he know she was dying? "I have to—uh—go check out some stuff, you know."

"Yeah?" Was that concern in his voice? Worry? Fear? For her?

"It's nothing big. Don't get your hat in a twist."

He laughed weakly. "That's *pantyhose,* dummy . . . don't get your pantyhose in a twist."

Aeryn felt laughter and tears inside, so close that she couldn't separate them.

"I'll see you around."

"Sure. Whenever they zip my brain back in and let me out of here, right?"

"Right." She rose. Searched for words that wouldn't come. "See you, Crichton."

"Sure thing."

She walked unsteadily to the door. No one even bothered to give her a second glance. As far as they were concerned she was dead already—dead even though she was walking. At the door she turned, unable to leave without saying something, anything.

His eyes were locked on hers.

He knew. Had to know that she was dying. He couldn't just have lain there and not heard her conversation with Jansz.

She ran back to the bed, pressed her lips briefly to his, and hurried from the room.

Her last memory was of his tear-filled eyes.

For Aeryn Sun the time for tears was past. She didn't know how much time she had before the neurotoxin Vurid had injected her with paralyzed her nervous system and stopped her heart. It could be several days before she died. But she knew she did not want to die inside a stupid hospital inside a stupid tin can.

Aeryn left the apothecary and walked as steadily as she could towards the launch deck. She was a Sebacean. She would end her life in the same place it began. Between planets, in the cold light of the stars that had watched over her birth.

The Nomad flotilla drifted in space, lazily orbiting the blue supergiant. Inside the trader flagship, the crew had finally dispersed, drunk and disorderly in a dozen languages, to their own unremembered pleasures.

Only two remained.

Jansz and Chiana were alone in the hydroponics garden, watching the stars, companionably smashed on the nectar of Vurid's passing.

Chiana hung upside down by her knees from the same branch she had been sitting on only moments before. "Y'know," her voice wobbled, "I haven't done this for . . ." She made an upside-down frown. "Actually, I don't think I've ever done it."

Eyeball to crawling, upside-down eyeball, Jansz studied the too-pale Nebari woman closely.

"Why," he asked as length, in a very loosely controlled trio, "is one even bothering to talk to you at all?"

"Know wha'cha mean," was Chiana's rejoinder. "Know 'xactly wha'cha mean. I mean, 's not like you know me or anything. I'm a complete X factor to you. I could be anyone."

Jansz thought about this while studying the inverted face a hand's breadth from his own.

"I can tell you I'm not, though. Anyone else, I mean. I mean, I'm me, if you . . . uh . . . see what I . . . Jansz, darling, why do the backs of my knees hurt? And . . . why are you upside down? And . . . oh, yes . . . why aren't we dead? I mean, we've all ingested Vurid's neurotoxin, haven't we? Is it the fruit?"

"Of course it's the fruit."

"Oh. So it's not just a good guzzle then?"

"You remember one's speech concerning species and symbiosis? It happens with fruit as well as people. The fruit on this tree contains proteins that mate with the proteins in Vurid's toxin. Eat some fruit and you don't die—you just get very, very . . . happy."

Jansz belched suddenly. Four blasts of sulphurous air.

Chiana yelped in surprise and fell out of the tree.

"Oh," said Jansz. "One is terribly sorry."

"You know, for a legendary trader and sometime murderer, you don't half apologize a lot." Chiana began to giggle.

Jansz wondered whether Chiana was laughing at him or with him.

He began to laugh. He shook.

He quaked.

He thundered.

The trunk of the fruit tree acquired half a dozen cracks where Jansz gripped it with one set of forearms while he wiped steaming tears from his own eyes with the remaining hands.

Chiana crawled a short but prudent distance away, then plonked herself back down on the velvety grass. Jansz was a dangerous fellow to be around. He weighed as much as one of Moya's pods. It wouldn't do to be in his way if he happened to stumble and fall . . .

Suddenly Jansz stood. Chiana felt the ground move. He looked around the garden, not appearing to see Chiana or Vurid's bier or any of the trees and shrubberies.

Chiana studied him closely.

He was looking at things that weren't there—he was seeing through the eyes of his Compound.

Eventually Jansz looked at her.

"Aeryn Sun has taken her Prowler and left the ship."

"Do you want me to follow her for you? Get her back?"

"No." Contact with his peripherals seemed to have sobered Jansz up fast. "Aeryn Sun wishes to die in space. I do not see any reason why she should not do this. You may, however, take a ship and follow her, to recover the Prowler when she has no more use for it."

Chiana nodded clumsily. "Okey-dokey."

Jansz looked puzzled.

"It's just something that . . ." Chiana hesitated. "It's just something that Crichton used to say. It's nothing. Forget it. I'll go now."

"Please do. Your company is well meaning but also confusing. You are of the Moya-gestalt. One has not yet decided whether to hold all of you responsible for the actions of Aeryn Sun. This notion of individuality is new. One must consider it fully before taking action. And . . . one would like to be alone with one's father."

"I understand." Chiana got unsteadily to her feet and wobbled off towards the hydroponics access tunnel. But there was nothing unsteady about her resolve. She knew what she had to do. Chiana had some friends to save.

Rygel woke first. He lay quietly, trying to order his scattered thoughts. Slowly, events came back to him.

He remembered the attack, the hideous sensation of being crushed in Moya's convulsions. And he remembered losing his ear. His ear—

Stubby fingers clutched his head. Both ears were intact. He felt relaxed and refreshed, incredibly well. Invigorated. He rubbed his head and became aware that he felt slippery. He was covered in some sort of gel.

Tiny, jelly-like organisms with translucent skin and hair-like tentacles were all over him.

And they tickled.

He giggled.

The gel-like things pressed lightly against him and

he was aware of something slippery pressing against his ears. No, it was pressing inside his ears. Rygel felt dizzy as he realized that he had been breathing in the gel-like things with every breath. *They were inside him.*

He sat up, horrified. Panicked, he thrashed his arms and legs around wildly.

Light flickered through the gelmass, a display like tame lightning, as Re, knowing that their job here was finished, slowly withdrew and parts of the gestalt died.

Rygel experienced an astonishing range of emotions in quick succession: love, laughter, guilt, remorse, anger, fear, terror, and hatred all played tag in his mind. He shivered uncontrollably.

The lightning flickered again, and then faded. The gelmass sloughed away from Rygel's body. He felt calm again and, briefly, a great sense of wellbeing.

Then the questions came. Lots and lots of questions. But they all boiled down to one. What the frak had been going on? It was a good question—one he had no answer to.

He heard someone stirring. Nyaella was waking too. Rygel watched in amazement as the same beautiful light display flickered across her body and then faded to nothing as the gelmass sloughed away from her, decayed and died. He felt his heart leap at the sight of her.

She sat up and rubbed her eyes.

"Rygel, are we all right?" she yawned. "I had such terrible dreams."

"Me too," Rygel replied, sleepily. "Do you recall what happened to us?"

"We were under attack in Moya. Then . . ." She shook her head. "I just don't know. Do you?"

"I just woke up myself," he answered. "Covered in slime!" He listened for a few moments. "Do you hear anything?"

"No."

"Neither do I." He paused. "Moya's very quiet. I think we should go and investigate. Find out if there's any damage."

She looked at him coyly.

"Can't that wait a little while? Everything seems fine."

Nyaella came over to his side. She put her arm around him and held him tight.

"Do you remember that time at the Moon Pool when your father was still Dominar?" she asked.

"Oh, yes . . . but it seems so far away now," he replied, suddenly embarrassed.

"I know a way we can make it seem closer," she said and pressed her lips against his.

Rygel relaxed; felt her body, warm and pliant against his, and surrendered to the moment.

Aeryn lay back in the flight seat and studied the stars. They twinkled sedately overhead, cold and steady points of hard brilliance. She closed her eyes. It was all right now. She was out here. Where she needed to be.

She'd felt the first wave of dizziness as she entered the launch deck. Skiffs had been ranged in a long line before the airlocks, cranes and weapons systems unshipped and ready for service. Aeryn had sneaked into the bay, grabbed the nearest likely looking weapon—a welding torch—and walked unsteadily towards her Prowler.

"Hey, you." She waved the torch at the technician unclamping the refuelling line. "I'm not in the mood for small talk. You've got three seconds to vanish or you're toast."

The technician vanished.

The ease of her escape surprised her—until she remembered she was dying.

Again she wondered how long it would take. The dizziness seemed to come in brief waves, in which she found movement difficult. But the fits seemed to last only seconds before passing. Would they get worse? She had studied accounts of people who had been infected with neurotoxins. Some had taken days to die, their bodies slowly shutting down as their nervous system crashed uncontrollably. Was that what was in store for her? Drooling paralysis and eventual suffocation when her autonomic system stopped?

Now the stars moved steadily by outside the canopy of the gun skiff and Aeryn allowed herself to drift back in the seat, back through her memories of Peacekeeper life, back through her memories of life on Moya . . . life with Crichton . . . with John . . .

It was good that he would live.

Aeryn felt an unfamiliar sensation briefly touch her mind. What was it he always said? *Grudges and gagh are for Klingons. Revenge is a dish best thrown in the trash.* She understood grudges, but gagh? She'd asked him what gagh was once. He'd told her it was worm soup.

D'Argo and Zhaan slept on, swaddled by Re, but still troubled by dreams.

D'Argo stared at the body of his wife and at the

empty room in which his son had once slept. He roared
defiance at a universe that could so casually deprive
him of those he loved, at a universe that could, at a single stroke, make his life one of meaningless despair.

Was there no place for love in this world?

No place for love or trust?

As a warrior, he should have known the answer. But
he was empty inside and he didn't.

When the Peacekeepers eventually came, they found
him silent and staring beside Lo'Lann's body, with her
blood on his hands.

It didn't matter what happened to him now.

Zhaan lay beside the body of her lover and, in her
mind, heard him speak of love and tolerance. But, inside, she raged at a universe that deprived her of the
one she loved.

Was there no place for love in this world?

No place for trust?

As a Tenth-level priest, she should have known the
answer to that. But she was empty inside and she
didn't.

When the Peacekeepers eventually came, they found
her lover dead and his blood on her hands.

It didn't matter to her what she did now.

Re listened, puzzled. The healing of Moya was taking
far too long. Those parts of her that were so troubled
needed much more time. And time was in very short
supply.

Re knew that the moment was fast approaching
when they would have to leave the planet. The blue supergiant was growing more unstable by the second and

would, frighteningly soon, go supernova. Re knew they would have to act before Moya was ready, would have to protect her further, take her away and into space. Re concentrated its great mind, packed itselves tightly around Moya's hull as a protective shell, and prepared.

Aeryn drifted, through space, through memory. She was calm and peaceful. There had been some pain, of course, but that had passed. Her eyes were half closed, her heart rate very slow and her breathing shallow. But she felt a strange and comforting warmth. There was no panic, no anger, just acceptance.

She had expected the poison running through her body to cause her distress and to hurt a great deal. But it didn't.

She supposed she must be lucky.

But she was sure there was something she should have done. Something she'd forgotten to do . . .

Incoming transmission.

"Aeryn listen to me. It's Chiana. I'm on *Farscape* with Crichton. Activate your tracking beacon now. I'm sorry, Aeryn. I made a mistake. I have a cure for you. Activate your beacon so I can find you. We might all still get out of this alive."

Chiana.

Yes! That's right, now she remembered what it was. . . .

Kill Chiana.

Aeryn blinked the stars back into focus. More stars joined them. Instruments on her navigation board. She booted up the weapons.

"Aeryn, why have you activated your weapons systems? I've got Crichton with me. If you fire now you'll kill us both!"

Long past listening, Aeryn smiled dreamily. She was in another ship, a bucket seat that cradled her with loving arms, that touched her mind with its own, that let her see through its eyes and reach out with its peripherals.

As she reached out now with weaponclaws eager to catch and kill.

Dying, confused, she turned her Prowler to face her tormentor.

She prepared to fight.

To the death.

When Moya suddenly shifted her position, Rygel and Nyaella were thrown to the ground. They looked at each other in alarm.

"What the . . . ?" Rygel began, struggling to his feet.

Moya lurched again and he toppled over, landing in an untidy heap on top of Nyaella.

"Moya's moving," Nyaella said, wide-eyed.

"Yes," Rygel said, "but not of her own volition. It felt like something underneath us shifted. We'd better get to the bridge."

They waddled through Moya, bumping against her walls every time the great Leviathan shifted her position, eventually making it to the bridge. The stomach-shaped chamber looked more like an underwater cavern than ever.

But it was obvious to Rygel that he was not going to find any answers to what was going on here. Everything, even Pilot, was inert.

He tried anyway.

"Pilot, it's Rygel. Report on the status of Moya."

But there was no answer.

He tried again.

"Pilot, where is everybody? Where's D'Argo? Where's Zhaan?"

No answer.

"Pilot, what's happening?" He was aware of an increasing note of desperation in his voice. He hoped that Nyaella couldn't hear it. He tried to speak calmly. "Pilot. Respond immediately."

Moya started to rock back and forth alarmingly in response, but Pilot didn't reply.

Rygel frowned and his eyelids blinked over nictitating membranes. For the first time, he was aware of a fundamental flaw in his operational knowledge of the star-going Leviathan he'd so cleverly stolen. He couldn't speak to Pilot. And he couldn't control the ship.

Rygel's thoughts raced desperately. The bridge viewtank was empty. He couldn't see what was happening outside Moya. Effectively, he was blind. He reached for the manual controls, but they didn't respond. He just couldn't activate them. Something else seemed to have control of the ship. He fiddled pointlessly with the useless manual controls for a few minutes and then gave up.

He was close to despair and Moya was now shuddering, as though she were having some kind of fit.

"Pilot, help me," he said very quietly. And then he remembered something.

With great difficulty, he maneuvred himself to the front of the bridge. He was thrown about by the convulsions of the shuddering ship. Her walls and floor undulated and writhed. Eventually, he found the nodule he was searching for and pressed on it.

Nothing happened and he applied more pressure.

Painfully slowly, one of Moya's cameras cracked open.

Rygel could see that the ship was underwater and covered in the same jelly-like substance that had covered him when he had awoken.

He called to Nyaella and she lurched across the bridge to his side. They both stared out helplessly at the churning water.

Nyaella pressed against him and held tightly to his arm.

"What's going on, Rygel?" she asked in a tiny, frightened voice.

He could only shake his head.

Suddenly, the shuddering stopped and Moya headed for the surface.

Never had the gestalt entity that thought of itself as Re known such power. It struck the skin of its world travelling faster than it had thought possible.

The rock had no time to buckle: it melted, vaporizing instantly as Moya surged upwards into the waiting sky that blazed with blue fire.

CHAPTER 11

The Moya that rose from the ocean world, through the flames of the blue supergiant, was very different from the Leviathan that had been so close to death when she had crashed there.

She was still healing even as she moved, but she was now full of life. She and the gestalt entity that enveloped her erupted from the planet, tore through the layer of cold vacuum that surrounded them, punched a hole in the photosphere of the supergiant and emerged once again into the familiar light of distant suns. Her skin glistened, and sparking tentacles trailed from her. Within her skinsteel hull, new organs pulsed with life.

Staring out from the bridge at the flame-streaked sky, Rygel tried once more to discover what was going on.

"Pilot, report Moya's status."

"Moya is in excellent health. And so, I might add,

am I," Pilot replied promptly. "But there is something strange . . ."

Rygel whirled around.

"What? What is strange, Pilot?" he snapped.

"I'm afraid I don't know." Pilot paused. "Moya has recovered completely and yet she doesn't seem to be in complete control of herself. I can't access everything. It is most perplexing."

Rygel was uneasy and restless. His brow smoothed as he lost himself deep in thought. If Pilot didn't know what was going on, it was unlikely that he or Nyaella would be able to work it out. He decided to look around the Leviathan, to see if he could find the others.

He smiled at Nyaella and she moved to his side and fell into step with him. Together they left the bridge.

Re thrilled to flight. After being so long weighed down by water, the sheer exhilaration of soaring through space was unbelievably intense. The gestalt looked down at its planet and at the blue supergiant and realized it had escaped.

Re was hugging the Leviathan tightly, taking energy from her and, in a close and meaningful symbiosis, giving protection in return. Moya was almost a part of the gestalt.

Re considered its options.

It could remain with Moya, flying off to the unknown. Or Re could follow its original plan.

As Re pondered, a powerful, harsh voice broke into its thoughts.

"Are you ready to trade with one? It is time."

Momentarily, Re was startled. On the two previous occasions it had spoken with the trader, Re had initiated contact. That he knew where, and how, to find Re was something that would have to be thought about.

"We are not sure we wish to trade with one now. We need a little time to consider."

"There is no time. It must be now. Before the star explodes. If one is to take you offplanet, I repeat, it must be now."

So the trader didn't know where they were.

"We are no longer on our planet. We have escaped."

"How?"

"We have healed the Leviathan. We are free. We are in space."

The silence was deafening.

Jansz stood in the hydroponics garden and wept acid tears for a dear friend. Only now, cut off from his Compound and for the first time in a great many dekacycles truly alone, could he grieve.

The words of the thief, Chiana, rippled in his mind. *There's never enough time.*

"All the time in the world would not have been enough." His words fell softly, like his tears, but just as his tears ate steaming pits into the organic mulch, so his words ate tracks in his mind.

Jansz was not young, nor yet was he especially old. His species was possessed of moderate longevity. And probably more than reasonable insight. And Jansz himself was not the most innocent of people. A habitual criminal, he had stolen, fleeced, conned, and, when necessary, murdered his way across half the Uncharted Territories. He had produced in others losses ranging from simple baubles, easily replaced, to loved ones whose lives he priced well only for those who killed for money.

To think that in all that time, despite all that deprivation, he had never experienced a loss so great as this. The feeling coiled inside like a parasite, eating away at his self-control.

He wanted to shriek, to tip his skull back and scream a choir-voiced rage at the unchanging stars. Instead he wept quiet, bitter tears. He caught them upon his palm and clenched his fist about them, flesh searing as the acidic enzymes bit deeply.

The news that Moya had recovered and was in space had prepared him. When the voices of his Compound finally penetrated his consciousness and told him that the Leviathan had burst free from world she had crashed into and had now been sighted in solar orbit, Jansz decided what he was going to do.

He was going to kill those on board. All of them.

And he was going to do it right now.

Rygel and Nyaella wandered aimlessly along one of Moya's main arteries, deep in thought.

Rygel had only ever wanted the simple life.

To be Dominar and to be worshipped as a living god, loved by billions. Was that so much to ask of a cold and unfeeling universe? He sighed.

Nyaella turned to him at the sound.

"What's that?" she said.

His brow smoothed in consternation.

"Nyaella, we should have been together long ago. It just wasn't fair that we should have been kept apart. But now we have another opportunity. An opportunity to be together again. An opportunity for . . ." He shrugged. "I'd say happiness, but I'm sure that merely uttering the word will doom any chances we have."

Nyaella laughed. The sound sent thrills along his every nerve ending.

"You always were an incurable romantic," she said.

"Better that for a Dominar than the inbred neurotic who deposed me," he replied, with some warmth.

"Now, darling, don't be bitter. Whatever cousin Bishan's shortcomings may be, he is Dominar now. And for every door that's closed to you, another opens."

Rygel nodded in agreement.

Then they stumbled across Zhaan and D'Argo, lying side by side, still covered in the thick gel that Rygel recognized.

Nyaella shrank back.

"Are they dead?" she asked, in a tight voice.

Rygel leaned down and listened. He could hear them breathing and could see their chests rising and falling.

"No," he said, "they're only sleeping."

Overcoming his revulsion at the sight and feel of the gel, he shook D'Argo by the shoulder.

"D'Argo, wake up," he shouted. But the huge warrior didn't stir.

Rygel shook Zhaan, too, but to no avail. He looked back at Nyaella.

"Let's go back to the bridge and see if Pilot has made any progress or has any ideas on how to wake the sleeping beauties here," he said.

They retraced their steps to the bridge. They were breathless when they arrived.

"Pilot," Rygel finally stammered out, "what's the matter with Zhaan and D'Argo?"

"They are well, though they appear to be in deep sleep," Pilot replied. "But they may not be well for long."

"Why not?" Rygel asked, alarmed.

"Because," Pilot said, "we are about to come under attack. Trader-Prime Jansz has launched all his remaining gun skiffs with orders to destroy us."

"That," said Rygel, sighing wearily, "was not the answer I was looking for."

Aeryn blessed a universe that allowed her to escape in her own Prowler. She hadn't really been able to believe her luck when she'd found it still where she had left it, ready and waiting for her, with a clear run out from the flight deck.

She found herself murmuring words of encouragement to the machine and laughed. It was absurd to talk to inanimate objects. It was something Crichton did. It was very human.

She was shaken out of the strange fugue state she was lapsing into by the flash of gunfire brushing past her port side.

Chiana again.

"Chiana, I've told you already: you fly within a dench of me and I'll blow you out of the sky."

"Aeryn, listen to me. I've got John. I've got an antitoxin for you, but they're after me. They're after us all. They're going to . . ."

"No more chances. Say one more word and I guarantee you will not like my reply."

"But . . ."

Aeryn activated the targeting system and drew a bead on the glowing dot that was Chiana's craft.

Then, with her thumb covering the firing stud, she hesitated.

Chiana had said she was on John's craft. And she'd said that she had John with her. Aeryn knew that Chiana was an inveterate liar, but just suppose she was telling the truth this once. Aeryn knew she couldn't risk being wrong.

She shut down the weapons system.

Maybe it would be better just to put as much distance as she could between herself and that treacherous little snurcher.

Gunfire passed close by. That frelling Chiana, Aeryn thought. I warned her what I'd do. Weapons system active again, Aeryn looked around and was shocked to see the sky full of gun skiffs.

They were shooting at her—and at Chiana.

"Aeryn, help! They want to kill us all!"

Aeryn snapped her vessel into a smart roll, and the sleek Prowler responded instantly.

The skiffs closed in and gunfire boomed, beyond the canopy. Aeryn watched in fascinated horror as gunfire smacked into *Farscape* and it tumbled out of control, careering wildly towards her—on a collision course. She wrenched at the controls, putting her Prowler into a controlled spin. Ghostfire bloomed all around her, the blur of stars, the glistening shadow of—

Aeryn whooped for sheer joy.

Moya! She was alive!

But Aeryn's joy was short lived. At the same moment that she was warning Pilot that she was coming home, Chiana's ship brushed against her Prowler and they both tumbled out of control towards the oddly glistening Leviathan.

"Pilot, it's Aeryn. Do you read me?" Aeryn gasped.

"I've very little control of my Prowler, and I've been poisoned. I'm heading towards you and it may be a bumpy landing. Over."

There was no answer from Pilot.

Aeryn chewed her bottom lip and fought to stabilize her ship. If she collided with Moya, the result could be dreadful for the Leviathan. It would be like being shot in the gut by a fragmentation shell.

"Come in, please. This is Aeryn Sun calling anyone on board Moya. I'm coming in—and I'm coming in *hot!*"

The gun skiffs bore towards Moya relentlessly and without fear. What was there to fear from a defenseless Leviathan?

But was she defenseless?

As Jansz led the gun skiffs toward Moya, he realized something about the Leviathan was different. The ship *glistened*. He did not remember it doing that before. He remembered it strobing with color like an animal in distress.

Perhaps Moya had been injured during her attempted escape?

Yes, that must be it. The Leviathan was a living creature. Her hull texture looked like burnt flesh covered in salve. Smothered in a substance that glistened like jelly. Shreds of gleaming material extended in writhing clumps from the body—and Jansz did not remember that either.

So. Wounded, weak, unmoving: the living ship was a perfect sitting target. Jansz ordered the attack force to close in.

"Try not to hurt the ship too badly. There may be tradable salvage."

The first acknowledgements had just sparked across his comm when Jansz felt an incredible jolt shake his gun skiff. The skiff jerked sideways and it was only his own considerable inertia that prevented him from having his neck snapped outright.

Nursing a sudden blinding headache, Jansz interrogated his diagnostics. Some kind of power surge had flashed out from the Leviathan. Electromagnetic. All the unshielded skiff systems were down and out.

He was drifting blind.

No.

Not blind.

Reaching out for the comforting presence of his peripherals Jansz made contact with his Compound. At once he saw. Proxy existence through Compound was second nature to Jansz. Still, integrating the views of so many of his peripherals was a task he wasn't up to.

It was not that it was difficult—just that it left one so utterly drained. The universe fractured, became a crystal maze of different, often conflicting viewpoints. Sensory stimulation that bordered on overload.

Jansz's perception focused, narrowing even as his viewpoints multiplied. He became the ghostwalker of his ancestors.

Through other eyes he saw:

A sparkling energy pulse burst out from the Leviathan's glistening hull, a glowing web to catch many of his fleet. More than a dozen skiffs puffed into cold fire at the touch of the pulse. A further twenty ships suffered terminal system shutdowns and began to tumble in a straight line from whatever vector they had assumed immediately prior to the pulse.

Jansz's mind shuddered at the impact of a maze of light—countless carousel views of the sky. The Compound's reactions ranged from focused concentration to blind panic. Two ships alone seemed to avoid the blast, and they were already moving with clear lack of control.

The craft piloted by Aeryn and Chiana joined his own and a dozen others on a tumbling collision course with the drifting Leviathan. Jansz allowed a little of his hindbrain perception to drain from the supersaturated sponge that was his mind and ego.

Control.

One really mustn't lose control.

The Leviathan whirled closer and closer. Jansz clung to his crash webbing and closed his eyes.

Moya whirled closer, closer . . .

Impact, when it came, was devastating.

The pain was quite unbearable.

Higher brain functions shut down for some while.

Jansz awoke.

Something was wrong.

Something beyond the fact that he was lying in near-boiling water that had cauterized a gaping wound in the muscular skinsteel hull above his head.

Jansz blinked blood—the Leviathan's and his own.

The world stubbornly refused to oblige with a matching blank spot. Instead, all that happened was that his viewpoint shifted so that suddenly he was

burning, I'm
out of here I'm drowning get me

hurts I can't breath I can't

seeing through the eyes of another—a member of his crew jammed between shattered skiff and skinsteel wound, immolated as the engines splashed fire into the flooded compartment, crushed as muscular contractions sealed the wound.

Jansz tried to shut down his hindbrain.

Nothing happened.

Massive shock flooded the tiny area of his sensorium not already saturated with the views and feelings and experiences of others. Jansz uttered a hideous, solo groan that rose slowly to a deafening shriek. Something between understanding and sheer terror. His Compound perception was damaged. He couldn't control the view or emotional states from his peripherals. For the Trader-Prime, ego drowning in the deaths of dozens of his peripherals, the world had gone suddenly and completely insane.

Aeryn felt the impact but did not see it.

Peacekeepers did not, as a rule, believe in traditional deities.

That Aeryn Sun survived the impact with Moya proved that she was very, very lucky.

Aeryn's Prowler crashed into Moya, tearing a great wound in the skinsteel hull. Remarkably, the fighter wasn't too badly damaged.

Farscape came in at the same time, battered and a little bent, but fundamentally sound. The Leviathan did not notice—she was already unconscious, insensible from the pain of multiple crashes.

Aeryn took a little while to recover from the impact. Then, she hauled herself out of her Prowler, checking her limbs for damage. Air whistled past her and she hung on to the side of her craft until the wound in Moya healed sufficiently for conditions not to be immediately fatal. Slowly, the atmosphere stabilized.

She was suddenly aware of a lot of jelly-like material everywhere. What was it? She had no time to ponder it as four or five of the traders entered the companionway, weapons drawn. They saw her and immediately began to fire.

Aeryn turned and ran, slipping a little on a patch of the gel-like gunk as she twisted around a corner. She lost her balance and slid down an artery slick with the stuff. She fell, arms out and wheeling for balance, and landed in another chamber. It was damaged but the wound was sealed with Crichton's module.

There was no sign of Chiana, but leaning on the hull of the damaged skiff was a familiar figure.

"Crichton!"

Still weak, almost unable to walk, the human grinned feebly.

Aeryn lifted Crichton, but she couldn't move with him. Dragging him was out of the question. The sounds of thudding feet and harsh voices were approaching.

"Goons?"

"If by 'goons' you mean Jansz's traders, then yes."

"Alright. Where are we?" Crichton asked weakly.

"Somewhere near the cargo bay, I think."

"Fine. Stash me somewhere. Lose the goons and come back for me."

"I'm not leaving you again."

"Aw, don't go all gooey on me, Princess. I'll be fine so long as you shoot straight. Now get outta here."

* * *

Jansz's fractured world revolved dizzily, a spider-web of madly jerking crystalline images.

He felt himself shoot

(themshootthemallright)

at the same time felt himself hit

(wanttodienotlikethisnot)

by multiple gunfire.

Hunter and victim at the same time.

Time *after* time.

Four voices pulsed in armored throats, moaning as his body shuddered, jerking this way and that under wildly conflicting emotional instructions and ever more diverse perceptions.

Once he found himself looking at the same scene from three different angles. Both *watched* and *felt* himself die. He ran howling through tunnelled images.

When Jansz staggered onto the bridge, four energy weapons waving wildly in his hands, Rygel's immediate reaction was to panic.

Helium filled the control room.

Some part of Rygel knew this was not good. Not the most combustible of gases, helium nevertheless tended to combine spectacularly with the ion flux from certain old-fashioned types of energy weapons. Just such weapons, for example, as Jansz was waving madly at Rygel and Nyaella right now.

"Now look." *Oh, it was so hard to maintain a measure of gravitas when one's voice was sliding inevitably upwards in pitch.* "I know you must be very angry but I would like to point out that, as a Dominar I command the respect—and armies—of an entire planet."

The guns waved.

Jansz moaned.

"On the other hand," Rygel stuttered nervously. "I would also fetch a considerable sum, if ransomed."

Jansz's compound eyes rolled in different directions. He seemed to be looking everywhere at once. Rygel was sweating.

"Of course, I would have to be alive rather than dead,"—*the guns, don't point them over*—"I mean, the ransom would be so much larger . . ."

Jansz's fingers tightened the triggers.

His moaning rose to a howl.

"I know all the right people to contact." *Believe me, I know them.* "I could make it really easy for you to . . ."

Jansz suddenly convulsed. The weapons flew from his grasp, hit the walls and dropped into the water. His body thrashed. Arms flew outwards, fingers spasming uncontrollably.

Rygel and Nyaella glanced at each other—and then dived to retrieve the guns.

A moment later they rose to find Jansz frozen in place, his breath whistling hard through four throats.

Rygel and Nyaella had collected a gun each. Jansz had managed to retain the other two. Four guns were aimed squarely. Muzzles gaping. Counters reading *full charge.*

Jansz blinked; eyes crawled like beetles. "They're nearly all dead now. One can function properly again."

His words were addressed to several different places on the bridge, only one of which Rygel was actually standing in.

Rygel felt, purely as a matter of courtesy, he should

point out that the atmosphere contained an explosive emission. "If you fire one of your guns, we'll all die," he stuttered, as firmly as he could manage.

Jansz's massive skull whipped up and around, homing in on the voice. He stared directly at Rygel.

"A threat?"

"A warning. I'm afraid when I'm nervous I . . ."

"Rygel, put your gun down!"

Rygel glanced sideways. Was he seeing things? Something was very odd. "Nyaella, shouldn't you be pointing your gun at Jansz and not at me?" he asked.

"If you kill Jansz, I'll kill you."

"He's got a gun aimed at your head, Nyaella!"

"He won't shoot me."

And then it hit him. And Rygel felt the truth slam home, more deadly than any weapons discharge.

"I'm sorry, Rygel." Her voice was hard. Brittle as broken glass.

Rygel found the breath hammering in his throat. "The kidnap. The ransom."

"All staged. We work together, Jansz and I."

"But . . . but . . . *why?*"

"It's fun." Her answer was shocking, obvious, and simple at the same time. "And for revenge—which has been a long time coming. Surely, Rygel, you know something about revenge."

Rygel was unable to speak. His heart smashed against his ribs.

"I still do love you though."

Rygel looked up. Hope blossomed—and died just as quickly.

"It's just that right now, Jansz is better for me." Her eyes were smiling. "In all sorts of ways."

Jansz smiled. In a silken solo he said, "Heart-warming, to be sure, but fundamentally flawed."

It was Nyaella's turn to be confused. Her gun remained aimed at Rygel. Jansz's guns covered Rygel and Nyaella.

"Oh, yes," he continued. "I'm sorry to have to disappoint you, Nyaella. Our time together was delicious. But that was before you met the love of your life and decided to double-cross me."

"But I . . ." she began in reply.

"There's no point in denying it," he said. "Why else would Re change its mind about trading? You must have manipulated your friend here in order to preempt my deal with Re."

"You're crazy," she said. "I didn't. I wouldn't."

Rygel felt himself reeling in shock. This was all too much. The gunbarrel wavered uncertainly.

"Who's Re?" he managed to stutter out. Jansz smiled with all four mouths. Teeth whirled.

"Re," he replied, "is the entity who healed Moya, who protected—and still protects—you. This entity, or gestalt, was trapped on a planet that will shortly be destroyed. Trading with me was its only means of escape. Why else do you suppose one brought an entire fleet so close to such a mad star?" The smiles narrowed. "Re is a very powerful and clever being but it has reneged on the deal and you, Nyaella, are at the back of it."

"No," she replied, "I don't know what you're talking about."

"Enough. The time for denials is over. One is sorry, as one does have a soft spot for you, but now you must die."

Rygel felt a cold fist grip his stomach. He looked up, brows smooth, eyes furious. His gun snapped upwards in his stubby hand until it was levelled at Jansz's head.

Three other guns jerked upwards in response.

A sense of calm flooded through Rygel. Incredibly, he found himself smiling. The smile he made whenever he was about to get exactly what he wanted.

"I just want to make it clear that I wouldn't normally do this sort of thing, at least not in person. But right now," his voice rose in gurgling fury, "I find myself looking forward greatly to splashing your stupid brains across the room unless you put your frelling guns down at once. Do you hear me? At once."

There was a moment of shocked silence, and then everyone was shouting.

"Drop your gun or I'll kill him!"

"Both of you drop your guns!"

"Shoot me and she dies!"

CHAPTER 12

Re knew it was weaker now. Repulsing Jansz's attack had cost it dearly. Healing Moya's many wounds had cost a lot. Many had died.

Re could feel Moya taking back control of her body, taking responsibility for the lives within her, and it felt a surge of—what? Pride? Love? It didn't know. But it was a feeling of deep satisfaction, of achievement. It had healed and protected Moya. Re could not just allow Jansz to destroy what it had saved. Oddly, after all the time spent trying to find a way to survive, death now seemed unimportant. Re knew that the Leviathan would live because of its power, and that was enough. But Re also knew that Moya needed more time to take complete control, and Re would try to give her that.

Chiana loped easily along Moya's main artery. Behind her she could hear shouts and heavy boots thudding against the floor. And it was all mixed in with the sound of gunfire. And Aeryn.

Aeryn fighting for her life, calling to Chiana for help.

But Chiana had other plans.

The chief of them being escape.

She'd brought Crichton back and she'd also carried with her the fruit that could save Aeryn's life—assuming that Aeryn gave her the opportunity to speak without first killing her, of course. She felt, though she had reservations about this that she couldn't completely repress, that surely, this was the limit of her responsibility. After all, she had no weapon with which to defend herself, nor any hand-to-hand combat training to protect her from the traders—no, give them their proper name, pirates—who were ruthlessly hunting her down.

"Pilot! Can you hear me?" Chiana shouted into her comm. "Seal the port ventral artery! Do it now! Pilot. Answer me! Please."

But there was no reply from Pilot.

Instead, there was the blast of a sidearm. And it was aimed at her!

Chiana ran in earnest now, her legs pounding hard, her breath coming in ragged pants. She wondered why Pilot hadn't responded to her cry and then more shots drove all thought from her mind except the need to hide, to plan, and somehow take the initiative and go on the offensive.

She ducked into a side vein. The valve oscillated weakly and then jammed. Something was preventing it from closing. It occurred to Chiana that Moya might not be in complete control of her own body, that she might have sustained some damage in Jansz's attack, that she may not have recovered completely from the devastating illness that had threatened her life.

More shots echoed along the main artery, rippling past the half-closed valve. Chiana didn't think it would be wise to wait around and engage the pirates hunting her. She turned and started to jog along the vein, hoping that the shots were not causing any serious damage to Moya.

For a short while it seemed as though she had made it clear of the fighting but then she heard the dull thud of boots pounding relentlessly behind her. She increased her speed, trying to move as quietly as possible. She assumed that they must have heard the sound of her fleeing, the regular patter of her feet, the harsh gasps as she struggled for breath.

The sounds of pursuit grew closer. The terse, shouted commands and the monosyllabic responses bounced off the walls of the vein. She ran faster.

And then she stopped.

The vein just ended, stopped at a nexus from which a hundred or so smaller capillaries ran in all directions: upwards into the ceiling, down into the floor. The skin-steel walls here were pulsing gently. Too gently.

Chiana realized that she was in Moya's lungs and that her breathing was too shallow. There was a rush of bubbles with every pulse. There was water in Moya's lungs. Chiana assumed it must have got there when Moya crashed into the planet, but she didn't have time to worry about it because the voices were coming closer.

She looked around frantically for somewhere to hide. She studied the capillaries. They were small, very small. Much smaller than the arteries used as companionways aboard Moya. She supposed she could wriggle into one. But then what? She'd be trapped and in full view of anyone who looked in. An easy target. Unless—

Hyperventilating now, Chiana threw herself into the nearest capillary opening and found herself hip deep in warm water. She grabbed at the pulsing, rough, textured walls and forced herself under the water. When her three pursuers moved warily into the area a minute later, the chamber was empty.

Chiana stayed under the water as long as she could, feeling her lungs almost burst with the effort. Voices carried indistinctly through the water.

When the gun blasts came they were like the high-pitched shrieks of animals echoing through a thick fog. Shock waves rolled along the tunnel and the water started to heat up. For a few seconds it became unbearably hot, and Chiana had to resist an impulse to scream. She knew that if she did, she would inhale water and the game would be up.

Her mind started to wander and she felt dizzy. Chiana knew that she'd have to return to the surface if she was ever to take another breath. She leaned back against the wall to ease herself up and a sudden cry of panic welled up in her throat as she realized her predicament.

The blast of heat had caused the capillary walls to contract and she was wedged tight.

Not too far away, Aeryn cursed as she dodged the energy bursts that rippled past her and turned skinsteel walls to fused blobs of crisped flesh.

Aeryn had hidden Crichton by placing him as gently as she could in a wall recess and pulling folds of skin-steel around him. But no sooner had she done it than the gun-happy pirates had caught up with her and she had run again, leading them as far away from Crichton as she could.

Now she was caught in the open, in the still-sealed cargo bay, and she had nowhere else to run.

She moved swiftly into the shadows thrown by the textured walls of the hold and tried to melt into the background as four of the pirates, guns raised, followed her into the vast area. They were clearly intent on taking her down before assuming complete control of Moya, along with all the potential wealth that implied.

The pirates remained grouped together, eyes peering into the gloom, alert to the slightest movement, listening for the slightest sound. One of them waved a hand and the other three fanned out a little, in a rough semicircle.

Aeryn looked for something that would give her any advantage. She did have superior knowledge of the terrain, experience of the interior workings of the Leviathan. Most likely, her pursuers had never been on one before. That was an advantage.

Almost immediately, she saw what she was looking for a short dash away. The dark, familiar shape of the refuelling root loomed between her and the pirates. If she could make it without being seen, she might just have a chance. The plan was insanely dangerous, but right now Aeryn didn't have any choice.

She considered how to distract the pirates. It would have to be the oldest trick in the book. She knelt down and felt around on the floor. There was always a little debris in the cargo hold and she quickly found a small, hard, flat disk. She had no idea what it was, but it suited her purposes perfectly.

She took a deep breath and then threw the disk hard across the chamber. It clattered against a far wall, dropping to the floor with a faint metallic clang. All the pirates whirled around and fired shots in the direction of the sound.

Keeping low, Aeryn hurled herself across the few yards that separated her from the refuelling root and crashed against it gratefully. She couldn't believe she hadn't been spotted, but no one fired at her or yelled out. She waited a few seconds and then started to climb.

The pirates walked warily toward the source of the noise. Finding nothing, they turned and peered around. Aeryn was right. None of them had ever been in a Leviathan before and, although common sense told them that they were in a chamber of some importance, they had no clear idea of what it was.

Consequently, when one of them spotted their quarry climbing a trunk-like growth clinging to one arched wall, none of them gave a moment's thought to the possibility that she wanted to be seen.

Aeryn climbed and four guns flamed as one.

But Aeryn was no longer there.

Hanging on grimly to a loading vine, she swung free of the refuelling root subsidiary junction and hurled herself through the flickering darkness.

A split second later, the gun blasts burrowed into the wall where she had been, with spectacular—and lethal—results.

The refuelling system exploded violently with a great whoosh. Huge gouts of flame billowed across the cargo hold, completely engulfing the pirates, killing them instantly. At the same time the explosion tore a ragged wound in Moya's skinsteel hull.

Aeryn turned for a second as she hurtled through the cargo bay access valve. In the wild, hurricane-filled moment before the valve closed she saw four charred corpses fly out into the void. Then the valve shut tight and the airflow stopped.

Aeryn relaxed her grip on the loading vine and fell heavily on to the deck.

I must be mad, she thought, utterly mad.

Then she heard a noise behind her and turned.

She saw Chiana, dripping wet, hair plastered along her jaw, the skin of her hands and face red and blistered where they had brushed against the fleshy sacs of lungmesh.

Chiana. Dislodged by the explosion. Alive.

Good, Aeryn thought and raised her gun, because I've got a score to settle with her.

Then, for Aeryn, time slowed. She didn't know if it was the poison or shock but she couldn't seem to fire her gun and the moment stretched out. She saw Chiana turn at the sound of footsteps, saw the two pirates step into the artery, guns coming to bear on Chiana. She knew she must have yelled because Chiana looked across at her for a second, her face a mask of fear.

She's just a girl. The thought flashed across Aeryn's mind and, without thinking about it, she threw her gun towards Chiana's outstretched hand.

She instantly regretted it. Thoughts tumbled into her head in quick succession as the rifle sailed through the air.

She shot John.

I can't trust her.

What am I doing giving her my weapon?

Suddenly, she knew the answer to that. It wasn't because she wanted to and it wasn't because she thought it would save her life. It was because it was what John would have done, because he gave his trust. And in that moment, Aeryn felt a powerful emotion rip through her mind, through her heart. The understanding that there was something that the human could teach her after all.

Chiana jumped as the gun slapped into her hand. Her finger curled around the trigger. She knew that skill didn't come into the equation. She would point and fire and not worry about the consequences.

Aeryn lay flat and watched as Chiana turned to face the two pirates whose own guns were already spitting flame. A scream ripped from her throat as she gunned them down.

CHAPTER 13

Re felt Moya's pain as the skin of the hull split and flame erupted out into the void of space. It moved to soothe and heal, spreading itself across the raw wound. It was very weak now but willingly sacrificed more of itself to ease Moya's distress.

It sensed that all was not well within Moya's respiratory system and seeped gently into the interior of the great ship to seek out and resolve the problem. It knew now that life was the greatest gift it could give, and it would give it until it was no more.

Back in the badlands.

Captain Rae SoeuDva allowed the contours of her smoothly angular face to form into a frown. On any normal day such a display of her inner feelings would not be allowed. Today was different. Today the Peace-keeper Tenth Operations Squadron was engaged in far from tactical maneuvers.

No war this, but a rescue. A mission of mercy.

SoeuDva stood, feet planted foursquare upon the bridge of the PK frigate *Bellatrix,* summoning her first officer with a slight gesture of her hand. "Jaen. Tell me again about this signal."

Jaen Evbow was a stark comparison to her commanding officer. Spare where SoeuDva was ample, her hair short, yet still holding a hint of a flip that, though within spec, was an indulgence the Captain would never allow herself.

"A reg-one SOS, Captain. Codes are old but they check out."

"The *Bellerophon?*"

"The very same."

"Thank you." SoeuDva's mind raced. An experimental ship, *Bellerophon* had been posted missing more than three cycles ago. No trace of her had ever been found. Now this. A Lifebuoy signal.

Survivors?

It seemed unlikely.

What seemed more likely was that the *Bellerophon* had been 'jacked and re-dressed, disguised from prying eyes while whoever now owned her dissected her for the secrets she contained. A quick way to steal a march on the Peacekeepers. Hence the Tenth Operation Taskforce.

No one seriously expected survivors. She checked back with Fleet Command. They expected a trap, or an accidental buoy launch. Either would be useful. One might get them the *Bellerophon* back, and that would mean a nice fat promotion, while the other . . . well the other could yield almost any dividend. If you put the right spin on it.

"Time to coincident spatial position?"

Evbow did not need to check with her staff. "Six minutes."

"Sound alert."

The klaxon fired once. That was all. SoeuDva ran a tight ship. Tension on the bridge changed not one iota. Her staff was well disciplined.

The bridge viewtank lit. The universe sprang to life, modelled precisely in the tank, replacing the dead grey flux of hyperspace that had existed there for the past seventeen days.

The tank contained a number of other objects. The nearest group was familiar—the fifteen ships of the Tenth Taskforce. The rest were not.

SoeuDva had a practiced eye. She estimated that more than a hundred ships of spectacularly diverse designs hung in space before her. None of them was a PK Lifebuoy. Trap, then. SoeuDva considered. The weapons were already primed, standard operation procedure when on grey ops. Firing time was optimal, a matter of seconds.

Tactical displays showed none of the unfamiliar ships had activated its weapons systems. Not a trap, then. Not an obvious one, anyway.

"Weapons, standby."

Evbow moved alongside. SoeuDva spared the slim woman a glance. "Opinion?"

"Nomads?"

"Concur. Illegals, do you think?"

"They're not exactly rushing to give us their registration numbers, are they?"

In fact the Nomad Flotilla as a whole had begun at last to respond to the Peacekeeper presence, hopelessly slow in terms of military finesse. About a dozen ships began to move smartly—in the opposite direction to the Taskforce.

SoeuDva inclined her head minutely. "Identification."

Thirty seconds later the good news came.

"It's Jansz." From the tone of her voice it was clear Evbow recognized the significance of that name.

"Is it now?" SoeuDva grinned wolfishly. "Fire up the main guns, then, Evbow, if you'd be so kind. Today's our lucky day. It seems we have a major criminal to arrest."

"Right away, Captain."

"I think a warning shot is appropriate. Weapons officer. Pick a target. Something small that they won't miss. Target the engines if possible, but you needn't be too careful."

If the Nomad flotilla had been less than prompt in responding to her presence, it reacted like a hive of bees to the sudden destruction of one of its smaller members.

"Evbow, make contact."

SoeuDva's exec nodded smartly. "Com-Officer, send this message: Captain SoeuDva, Tenth Operational Peacekeeper Taskforce to Nomad Trader Jansz. It is my great pleasure to inform you that you, and your scurvy fleet of fruit-sucking economic subversives, are under arrest. You have one minute to surrender or I will personally throw the switch on the weapons that will immolate you."

"You have a way with words, Evbow," SoeuDva acknowledged.

Evbow allowed herself a tight smile.

"I have my moments, Captain. Perhaps just a few, but I do have my moments."

For the record, it would never be possible to finally deduce who first opened fire upon whom. In the end, of course, it simply didn't matter.

For Rygel the first shot was paramount. Whoever fired first would have the best chance of survival. Everyone had a gun and everyone was waving it at everyone else. Jansz swivelled his between Nyaella and himself. Nyaella angled her weapon between Jansz and Rygel. Rygel whirled clumsily between one opponent and the next, trying to come to terms with the idea that Nyaella might really love Jansz.

Jansz, on the other hand, seemed quite capable of shooting either Nyaella or Rygel—preferably both.

Bearing this in mind, it seemed logical to assume Jansz fired first—but really, it made no difference.

Four guns fired.

The helium in the air ignited.

Flame blasted across the bridge.

Three bodies dropped to the flooded deck.

Silence. Then, one began to move.

Moya's skinsteel deck heaved beneath Aeryn as she tensed to jump. She swayed, grappling desperately for balance.

Chiana's gun—Aeryn's own gun, she reminded herself—was aimed at her. Not a particularly steady aim, nor indeed a more than average display of control. It was clear to Aeryn that Chiana was no gunslinger. The gun swung with the deck, back, fore, lock, no lock. Odds on a shot would miss, but you could never tell.

One lucky discharge and it wouldn't matter whether Chiana was a medal-winning sharpshooter or a dumb joe who couldn't hit an asteroid if it was hovering in front of her face.

The way Moya was bucking right now, it was all down to luck.

"Aeryn, wait!" Chiana cried. The younger woman transferred the gun to one hand while she scrabbled madly for something in her pocket. "I've got some fruit. I can save you!"

Aeryn scowled. *Fruit? What was the woman screeching about now?*

The deck swung again. Aeryn toppled.

Chiana lost her balance and fell also. Her hands formed involuntary fists—the gun went off.

Aeryn felt a hammer smack her between the ribs.

She flashed suddenly on

Crichton falling, falling to the deck of Jansz's ship, falling and groaning, surprise and shock, as blood emptied from him onto the deck and she rolled with the blow, mind clicked instantly to Peacekeeper mode, hunter-mode, her training unignorable, a night-black predator whirling in a the storm-dazzle of Moya's strobing lumoweed.

She dived across the intervening space to grapple and hold, to cry out in triumph and pain from armor-sheathed ribs as fingers locked around Chiana's neck, and squeezed, as Crichton struggled free of his hiding place to roll groaning between them, life's blood staining the gell-covered deck black—

Out beyond the dying supergiant, chromeblack flecks of metal surged towards a sea of neon graffiti—the

Peacekeeper Taskforce and the Nomad flotilla. One group bent on arrest the other on escape.

No quarter asked.

None given.

Weapon systems armed, and locked on..

Demands made.

Give us Jansz. He is wanted on forty-seven major indictments. Give us Jansz and we will not attack.

Answers given.

. . . don't know where he . . .

. . . to believe us! You've . . .

. . . think he may be . . .

. . . dead, they're all dead! . . .

And then the words were over, patience gone, the vast, inescapable mother-of-pearl wall producing shock and panic on both sides.

And the guns spoke—

And ships emptied themselves into the vacuum—

Brief stars blossoming—

Metal flowers coughing little seeds to their death as reactors ran wild, sirens blasting raucous noise into shattered eardrums that could no longer hear, displays blinking bright alarm into eyes that could no longer see.

The PK guns spoke again, coughing molten fire.

The Nomad weapons answered with furious, brutal light.

Ships began to explode. Space was filled with sudden bursts of light as a hundred Nomad ships tried to lose themselves in the sanctuary of the eternal night. They found only death, as PK hunter-killers sought them out, struck and unravelled them.

And then the rain of death found the Trader-Prime's

ship, snug and safe within its defensive fleet.

Energy weapons locked on.

The flagship blinked light from a dozen blind eyes.

Metal disintegrated, fell to liquid strings and lumpy vapor, instantly snuffed out in the icy reaches.

Engines blasted, reactor containment shot, the ship that had been home to Trader-Prime Jansz and Vurid Skanslav for more cycles than either would have cared to admit, erupted in a violent schism of light and matter.

The explosion was violent, incredible. Millions of tons of material transformed instantly into energy. For a few seconds a tiny sun burned where Trader Jansz's ship had been. The blast caught several more ships, Nomad and Peacekeeper, and they turned to vapor in a moment of time too short to measure.

Still, the fury of this blast was nothing compared to what was to come. The universe had one more shot in its stellar armory. Gravitational balance finally disrupted as its core-fuel ran out, the blue supergiant began its final collapse.

Supernova.

Moya knew what was to happen now: she had seen it before, as a child.

The process was simple: old, mad, and tired, the star's core had finally caved in, its fuel exhausted. Moving at one-tenth of the speed of light, the star's exterior would collapse, hit what remained of the core and bounce—and blast the outer layers of the star away in a gigantic explosion, big enough to be seen across half the galaxy.

As the heart of the star collapsed to form first a

whirling mass of iron and then a superdense neutron star, the photosphere would expand outwards in all directions forming a new nebula, light years across, destroying anything in its path, reducing all matter, any matter, to fundamental particles.

Moya herself. Her crew. The battling fleets of spacecraft. All would be destroyed. Moya stiffened her resolve.

She would not allow her friends to die.

Re had made Moya whole, her body healed and much of her strength coming rapidly back. Without waiting for instructions, she went into StarBurst, tore a hole in the universe and dived again towards the dark side of the sun.

For the second time, Rygel was shocked to find himself alive aboard a fleeing Moya. The Hynerian stood weakly on legs that trembled even more than they would under the pull of normal gravity. He lowered the bundle he carried reverently to Moya's skinsteel cargo deck. He shook.

And he sat beside the only Hynerienne, apart from his mother, whom he had ever truly loved. He closed his eyes, opened his mouth and uttered a wail of despair that would have chilled the coldest of hearts.

How could it all have been for nothing?

How could life be so cruel?

Rygel lowered his stubby fingers to touch her perfectly wrinkled brow, her cold, closed eyes.

Perfect. Even now.

You might almost think she was asleep.

Pain bloomed within him, grew swiftly, an impenetrable wall against which he battered himself over and over again.

If only he had never rejected her.

If only she had never hated him.

If only they had never met.

If only—

"I am a *Dominar!*" Rygel's voiced cracked, and he started to sob uncontrollably. Then he stiffened his resolve, pulled himself up to his full height and continued. "And I order you to give her back!"

The universe, as it had always done, maintained an icy indifference in the face of Rygel's absurd demand. And Nyaella, despite all his tears and entreaties, remained quite dead.

As the blue supergiant underwent final collapse, Re shuddered, taking the full force of the blast, deflecting it from the smooth hull of the Leviathan. And they slowly started to die.

Zhaan and D'Argo both awoke from their bloody dreams, the awful images that had haunted them for so long, stark and vivid in their minds.

The gel-like substance that coated their bodies fell away and they looked at each other, puzzled expressions on their faces. Then they looked out at the horrific scene as the star entered the final phase of its destruction.

How could they possibly survive the awesome power of the explosion?

Moya knew.

At a fraction of the speed of light, Moya swam down into the supergiant.

She raced towards the collapsing core, and the universe ripped apart to let her pass.

Behind her hovered the boiling wave front that was the exploding photosphere, the shredded mass of rubble that had once been a living world and two fleets of spacecraft; already dead, awaiting the fiery immolation that was only moments away.

Before her the steep gravity well of the infant neutron star. Dark and greedy, it reached for her with claws of gravity. Moya had been born to a star such as this; it held no fear for her. Just exultation.

She uttered a sound that no living ears could ever hear.

Life and death so intimately bound they were a single state of being.

Moya uttered a prayer to unknown gods and drove downwards, fins tightly furled, a flame-stitched arrow moving at one-tenth of the speed of light, to tear a hole in the blue star's black heart and vanish from the universe altogether.

CHAPTER 14

For Crichton, time contracted. Memory collided, a whirlpool of emotions and knowledge not his own.

He heard guns fire—

Felt projectiles tear into flesh—

Saw ships tear themselves into so much stellar trash—

BOOM-BOOM

The thready pulse of his own heart . . . quasar regularity slowing, speeding, slowing again as his body succumbed to the pain and shock of his injury.

He was tough.

He had to be.

Wasn't he the son of Jack Crichton?

But he could not live forever.

No man could.

BOOM-BOOM

Vagrant thought: that such an improbable series of events could ever have come to pass . . . that the whole gig just reminded him of so many desperately twentieth-century flicks that he couldn't put a name to them all. Maybe life did imitate art. *Pulp Fiction.* True Romance.

Tell it to Tarantino, baby.

BOOM-BOOM

Random memory collisions: Rygel holding the body of the Hynerienne he had won and lost and won again only in death—

BOOM-BOOM

Fleeting images of otherwhere: Aeryn, head cradled by Chiana, corralling her strength for a last effort—to swallow the mouthful of fruit, the juice staining her lips and chin—

BOOM

Dissolution of self: Zhaan and D'Argo suffering from a *major* collective guilty conscience as Moya rescued them just moments before the world on which they were trapped vanished forever from the universe—

BOO-

His heartbeat. Crichton could hear his own heartbeat.

It was OK.

It was OK, he was going to be

boomBOOMboombmbmbmbmbmbbbbbbbbb————

So Crichton died, his heart suddenly mute, the voice of his blood gone to silence; body cooling as molecules began their final, inscrutable journey to decay.

The last of Re slipped out from Moya's lungs and surrounded the still, huddled form that was John Crichton, the human astronaut from a place called Earth. Re cared for nothing now but healing and so seeped, agonizingly slowly, along a trail of blood and shock, seeking out the patient. Re slowly enveloped the human, entered him and began the process of repair and renewal that would inevitably lead to Re's own extinction.

One life for another. In this case, it was a noble exchange.

EPILOGUE

Crichton opened his eyes. Thanks to Re, he was alive. The shattered blue supergiant was many light years behind them now.

All his friends were clustered around his bed: D'Argo, Zhaan, Chiana, Rygel, and, of course, Aeryn. Pilot, too, was present. And around them all was the comforting skinsteel mass of Moya.

"Tell me about Re," Crichton asked. "I wish I had been able to thank . . . it? . . . for saving my life. What the heck is Re anyway?"

"Re was a gestalt organism," Zhaan explained. "A highly enlightened and very powerful being. It absorbed the infection that was killing Moya, and saved all our lives. It even deflected some of the solar radiation from the supernova. And it not only saved your life, but actually brought you back from the dead." She paused. "A breathtakingly selfless thing to do. Re gave its life that we could live."

"It was a far, far better thing," Crichton murmured to himself.

"What?" Aeryn asked.

"Nothing," Crichton replied, "just something that someone in a galaxy far, far away once said."

They looked at him with puzzled expressions.

Rygel sniffed back a tear.

"But even Re couldn't save Nyaella," he mumbled.

"I'm sorry, Rygel," Crichton said, sympathetically. "I know how you feel."

Rygel sniffed again, this time disdainfully.

"How can you possibly understand," he replied, sadly.

Crichton's smile became wistful.

"Because I've lost people I love, too."

Rygel gazed at the too-large, too-pale human hand resting upon his own handsomely wrinkled, leathery, green fingers.

He did not pull it away.

Moya lay quietly in space, listening to the stars—the regular beat of the pulsars, the strange whispers of ancient giants, and the awful silence of black holes.

ACTION FIGURES

SCI FI™

Now Available Through

TOY·CLUB

WWW.TOYVAULTTOYCLUB.COM

Phone#
606.523.9102